SAVAGE HELLFIRE

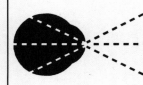

This Large Print Book carries the
Seal of Approval of N.A.V.H.

SAVAGE HELLFIRE

JORY SHERMAN

THORNDIKE PRESS

A part of Gale, Cengage Learning

GALE
CENGAGE Learning™

Detroit • New York • San Francisco • New Haven, Conn • Waterville, Maine • London

GALE
CENGAGE Learning™

Copyright © 2010 by Jory Sherman.
Thorndike Press, a part of Gale, Cengage Learning.

Thorndike Press® Large Print Western.
The text of this Large Print edition is unabridged.
Other aspects of the book may vary from the original edition.
Set in 16 pt. Plantin.

LIBRARY OF CONGRESS CATALOGING-IN-PUBLICATION DATA

Sherman, Jory.
  Savage hellfire / by Jory Sherman. — Large print ed.
    p. cm. — (Thorndike Press large print western)
  ISBN-13: 978-1-4104-3228-5
  ISBN-10: 1-4104-3228-9
  1. Large type books. 2. Savage, John (Fictitious
character)—Fiction. 3. Gunfights—Fiction. 4. Revenge—Fiction.
5. Murderers—Fiction. 6. Brigands and robbers—Fiction. I. Title.
PS3569.H43S284 2010
813'.54—dc22   2010036517

Published in 2010 by arrangement with The Berkley Publishing Group, a member of Penguin Group (USA) Inc.

Printed in the United States of America
1 2 3 4 5 6 7 14 13 12 11 10

For Ted Salinas,
wherever you are.

1

John Savage looked across the shadowy creek at the old diggings, so silent and forlorn in the soft mist of morning. His horse whickered uneasily as if it, too, could feel the eeriness of the place. The clouds were low and the creek was only partially visible under the blanket of fog, the wisps of vapors that rose from the chill waters like ghostly feelers from something buried there.

The packhorses snuffled through rubbery noses. John's horse, Gent, a rangy gelded trotter with three white stockings and a small blaze on its forehead, nickered uneasily in the quiet.

"You goin' to sit there all day and gawk, Johnny, or do we ride acrost?"

Ben Russell held the lead ropes of the two packhorses. He was riding a fresh-broke Arabian mix he had named Rusher, because the two-year-old was as frisky as a colt and always wanted to run and lead. Ben fought

7

him tooth and nail to break him of his bad habits. Rusher had a dull russet coat with a splash white blaze on its forehead. Ben said it had turned white from a thunderbolt and most of the electricity was still inside the horse.

John turned his head to look at Ben, a drift of brown hair on his forehead, hat tipped back slightly, his eyes dark as kohl.

"Spooky," John said softly.

"Ain't no ghosts here, Johnny. You got to get those things out of your head." Ben's eyes seemed to burn through the mist. He and John had been through a lot together, to hell and back, he thought sometimes, and now it was time to get a fresh start in life. Maybe, he thought, to start all over as they had planned.

"Their spirits are here, Ben," Savage said, his voice solemn, pitched to a prayerful softness, as if he was just entering a church.

"Aw, John," Ben pleaded, a note of impatience in the soft whine of his voice.

John clucked to Gent and ticked his tender flanks with both spurs. The horse stepped gingerly into the creek, adding new notes to the soft and lazy gurgle of the stream, the cold stinging his hocks so that he waded across quickly, his hooves splashing water halfway up all four legs. Ben followed with the two packhorses, roiling the waters until they filled with sand and, he thought as he looked down, the glittering dust they sought, the tiny gold flecks swirling like fireflies in the black dolomite.

But the creek was dark and murky, and the sun was still harbored behind the mountains to the east, with only its pink and salmon tinge in the pastel clouds as faint as an old woman's blush.

John looked up toward the cliff beyond the beach, but the fog was still too thick for him to see the entrance to their old mine, the one he and Ben had been working in when Ollie Hobart and his henchmen had attacked the mining camp and murdered all of them along this very creek. Killed were his mother and father, his sister, uncle, and everyone else. Only he and Ben had survived the slaughter because they were in the mine and unarmed. But they had seen all the horror, seen the faces of the men and heard their names called out during the shooting.

An eerie sense of foreboding crept into John's senses as he looked back at the creek, the tendrils of mist steaming off its surface like the bony fingers of those who had died there, their blood soaking into the gravel and sand along the banks.

"Don't go through it again, John," Ben said.

"I'm not," John said, a little too quickly, he thought. A lie, quickly spoken, but a way to quell the anger rising in him like the mercury in a thermometer, blood-red and as fierce as it was on the day he witnessed the bloody slaughter of his family.

"Maybe, we should just start our ranch up yonder and forget about that old mine."

So, John thought, Ben was spooked, too. He looked over at him and saw the blood-less skin behind his beard, the slight quivering of Ben's lips, the doubt flickering in his eyes like the fog shadows that littered the ground like the cast-off garments of dead men and women. And a little sister, robbed of life before she was dry behind the ears.

"We've got a week before the boys get our beeves up there," John said. "Let's make it count and see if we can strike some color."

"My heart ain't in it, John," Ben said. His brother had died there, too, with all the rest.

"Then put your muscle in it. Let's unpack those panniers, set up our tents, and store our gear up in the cave."

"I'll find us a place to unload," Ben said, and pulled the packhorses behind him as he rode beyond the place where they'd set up their old, original camp.

"Not too far," John said, as he looked down at the ground, as if seeking traces of the horror left there over two years before.

"I'll pick a place we wasn't," Ben said, and headed upstream, trying not to look at the place where they had all pitched their tents, lived, worked, eaten, drank, and played cards together, getting out the gold, until that fateful day when Ollie Hobart and his men had ridden up on them and started blasting with their rifles and six-guns. He could not see where the tent stakes had been, but he remembered, and he cringed inwardly as he rode along the burbling stream. He did not look up at the rimrock, nor at the cave where he and John had been working that day, unarmed, unable to help, unable to stop the slaughter. They had carried that day with them, and he knew it was still with them, and on them, and deep inside them.

But John had wanted to come back, work the claim, live up on the tabletop behind the bluffs, and raise cattle, build a home, maybe look for a wife.

Ben had not gone far when he heard the unmistakable sound of a crashing rock and the grating sound of sliding gravel. He reined up and turned to look back at John Savage.

John's hand was a blur as it dove for his six-gun, and before Ben could gulp down his fear, he heard the snick of the hammer being cocked. John was hunched in the saddle, his pistol barrel leveled at the cave entrance, ready to shoot. Dust rose in the air just beyond the cave adit, and trailed down behind a jumble of loosened rocks that were still skidding down toward the sandy shore of the creek.

"What is it?" Ben yelled, his hand floating toward the jutting stock of his rifle.

John did not answer. He was still looking up at the black hole in the rocky face of the bluff, through the lingering veils of mist, the wisps of smoky floating patches that still clung to the creek and hugged the mountain.

Ben had seen it before, but John's fast draw still caught him by surprise and filled his senses with wonder. He knew that the sight was dead on at the mine entrance and if anyone stepped out with a rifle or pistol, that person was liable to go down in the time it took to draw a quick breath.

"You're mighty touchy, John," Ben said as he rode up to his friend, expelling the quick breath he had held in his lungs until they started to burn. "It's just a bunch of rocks and some gravel."

John said nothing, but held his pistol steady, his eyes narrowed to twin slits as he peered through the rising fog. There was a stillness that sounded like thunder in Ben's ears, an awful stillness that comes when a man is about to die, or has just died. There was another thunder, waiting inside the barrel of that Colt in John's hands.

Then, they both heard it, a soft moan, a voice trying to sound a word.

"Yeopp," issued from the black hole of the cave.

Ben tensed and his fingers moved on the butt of his rifle, crawling like spider legs over the stock, ready to jerk it free of its scabbard.

"Help," the voice sounded again, forming the word.

It was a young voice. The voice of a girl or a boy from the sound of it.

"Help me," the voice cried, and there was anguish and pain behind it and through it as cold as icy shivers on a winter morning.

"Sounds like some kid," Ben said, loosening his grip on the rifle stock. "Can't see up there too good."

"You sit tight, Ben. I'm going to have a look-see."

"Be careful, Johnny. Might be some kind of trick."

John holstered his pistol, swung out of the saddle. He left his reins to trail as he walked toward the ladder set into the hillside. He climbed up to the sounds of moaning from inside the mine.

Ben heard it, too.

"Sounds like somebody's bad hurt, John."

John kept going, but turned his head and put a finger to his lips. Ben nodded. His horse whickered, and then began to paw at the ground with its right hoof.

"I got a gun."

John froze on the last step of the ladder. The voice was clear, but full of pain.

"You want help?" John said, tilting his head to throw his voice upward toward the adit.

"If you be friendly, yeah. Not one of them."

John wondered who "them" was.

"I'm coming in," he said. "If you shoot, that'll be the last thing you ever do."

"I-I won't shoot. You come on."

John climbed up onto the rimrock and came to the entrance on an angle, his right hand not far from the butt of his pistol. More groans from inside.

"You in there," he said, "can you walk? Or crawl?"

"I think my leg's broke. Stove up bad anyways. I might can crawl."

"You crawl on out here, then. And put your gun away."

He heard scrapings and scufflings from inside as he hugged the wall of rock next to the entrance. A few moments later, he saw the face of a boy emerge into the thin morning light.

"I ain't got no gun, mister," the boy said. "I was just a-bluffin'. You ain't goin' to kill me, are you?"

John walked over and pulled the boy out of the cave. His face was covered with bruises, a large purple one on his left cheekbone, another on his forehead. His nose had been bleeding and his upper lip was smeared with dried blood. Both lips were cracked and swollen.

"Who beat you, boy?" John asked, his voice soft, filled with concern.

"Them miners upstream," he said, and winced with pain. He grabbed his right knee and closed his eyes in pain.

"What you got up there, John?" Ben called through the rising mists.

"Bring me some water, Ben."

John knelt down and looked at the boy's leg. His pants were torn at the knee and he could see that his leg was scratched and swollen.

"I don't think your leg is broke," he said. "How'd you get that knee bunged up?"

"They — they hit me with a iron stob or a crowbar. I run off and they didn't chase me. Only laughed."

"Where did you come from to get into that fracas?"

The boy raised his hand, pointed a thumb up to the sky.

2

John heard Ben dismount and rummage through his things. There was an eerie quiet up on the rimrock. Little scraps of mist floated up toward him and the boy. He could not see Ben or the horses clearly, only fragments of hide and leather as the mist ebbed and flowed like curtains in a drafty room.

The sun began to breach the eastern rim of the front range, a red ball that nibbled at the morning mist and sprayed the pale blue sky with a tangerine glow, shooting rays of gold higher than the clouds. Ben clumped up the ladder and puffed over to John and the boy, his chest heaving and falling with the wheeze of a blacksmith's bellows.

"I brung some water," he said, holding out a wooden canteen.

John took the canteen, uncorked it, and held it out to the boy.

"Don't drink too much of this, son," John

said. "Just wet your mouth and take one swallow. In a while, you can have another squirt."

"Th-thanks," the boy said, and slaked his raging thirst. He started to take another pull, but John snatched the canteen away from him.

"How bad's he hurt?" Ben asked.

"Bruised knee, far as I can tell."

"It's all swolled up like a gourd," Ben said. "Might have some broken blood vessels from the looks of it."

"Can you climb down that ladder, boy, if I brace you?" John asked.

"I don't know," the boy said. "Can't put no weight on my leg."

"You'll just have to hobble down on one leg," Ben said. "I'll hold on to one hand and John will catch you if you fall."

"Just don't fall," John said.

The two men helped the young man stand up on one foot. Tears stained his cheeks and fresh ones flowed from his eyes as he stood there.

"It's throbbin' something fierce," the young man said.

"What's your name, son?" Ben asked. "I'm Ben and that's John got your other arm."

All three reached the rocky ground. The

18

boy was trembling, but stood on one leg as a long sigh escaped his lips.

"Th-thanks," he said. "My name is Whit. Whit Blanchett."

Ben's eyes widened into startled orbs popping out of their sockets like a pair of marbles.

"Blanchett?" Ben said.

"Uh, yeah," Whit said.

"John, ain't that the name we heard over to Cherry Creek some days back?"

"Something like that," John said. "You any kin to Argus Blanchett, son?"

"He — he's my pa."

Ben and John exchanged electric glances, spears of light colliding in midair like javelins. Whit saw the look and stiffened.

"John . . ." Ben started to say.

"Let it keep, Ben."

"Do you know my pa? Argus Blanchett?" Whit said.

"Not really," John said.

"Did you see him? He's been gone from home a spell."

Ben appeared ready to burst into song about Argus Blanchett, but a withering look from John deflated his cheeks and dulled his eyes back down to a pair of slits.

"Just show us where you live, Whit," John said, "and we'll take you back home."

19

"Me and Ma are settled up yonder," Whit said, pointing a finger toward the top of the bluff, above the mine entrance.

"You live up on the flat?" Ben asked.

"Yeah, we got a cabin Pa and me put up, and Ma's got her a garden started and Pa's down to Denver buyin' cattle. We're going to raise us some beef cows and sell 'em."

Neither man said anything.

"At least that's what Pa says."

"I can put some liniment on that knee, Whit," Ben said, "and maybe wrap a bandage around it. We'll take you on home."

"Ma must be pretty worried by now," Whit said.

Ben walked over to the horses and started rummaging in one of the saddlebags for his medical kit.

"What are you doing down here, anyway?" John asked as the boy sat down on a small boulder next to the creek.

The misty curlicues evaporated under the rising sun and rose to the clouds forming in the blue of the morning sky. John began to feel the warmth as the chill of morning wafted away on the pinions of a light breeze that sprang up from the east.

"Some men stole our milk cow two nights ago," Whit said, cocking his bad leg to take some of the strain off his knee. He looked bedraggled, John thought. "I follered 'em down to their camp up the creek. They had our cow. When I asked them to give it back, one of 'em took a stob and whooped me with it. I run off down here and hid in that old mine up there."

Ben returned with a tin of liniment and a roll of bandages.

"You say you live up yonder on the flat," John said. "Did you see our survey stakes?"

The boy looked startled. Color, a rosy hue, suffused his cheeks.

"Yeah, I reckon."

"Ben and I filed on that land some time ago and we mean to homestead it."

"Well, you can't," Whit said. "My pa claimed it."

"He has papers on it?"

"I don't know. Maybe. He said the land was ours. All of it."

Ben rolled up Whit's pants leg and liberally swabbed the bruised joint with a thick salve. Then he straightened the leg and bandaged it tight, but not too tight.

"You have to keep your leg straight and don't put no weight on it," Ben said. "I'll make you a crutch so's you can walk."

"You just lie here while we set up camp," John said. "Ben will make you that crutch and then we'll head up to the flat this afternoon."

"Yes, sir," Whit said. "My knee feels some better."

"Just lie still until we finish up making camp," Ben said, his voice wavering between sternness and sympathy.

"Yes, sir, I will," Whit said. "How come you're makin' camp here?"

John was walking away toward the horses, Ben ahead of him. He stopped and turned.

"We have a gold claim here, son. Had it for some time. We're just getting back to it."

"Where've you been?"

John didn't answer. He joined Ben and they led the horses upstream into the aspens and fir trees, began unloading the panniers.

"You goin' to tell that boy about his pa, John?"

"Not right off."

"When?"

"Maybe after I tell his ma."

"That ain't goin' to be easy."

"No, I reckon not. Meantime, Ben, just keep your thoughts to yourself."

"I ain't sayin' a word, John."

"No, but you're bustin' to blurt it all out to that boy."

"Me? Naw. I know how to keep a secret."

"Since when?"

"Well, for a long time."

John smiled.

"That boy's got grit, John. He might not take kindly to what you tell him about his pa. He's old enough to . . ."

"Ben," John said, some steel in his voice, "just back off the subject. I'll handle it."

"You might have to —"

"I don't draw down on boys, Ben."

"That young 'un's mite near a man."

"Enough, Ben. Let's get these tents up and the gear stowed. We've got a long morning and maybe an even longer afternoon."

"You can say that again, John."

John did not say it again, but they worked and made their camp in the shade of the trees, set out their pans and rockers, picks and shovels. One tent stored the dynamite, caps, fuses, extra lamps, ammunition, and foodstuffs.

Ben cut a forked limb from a lofty spruce and began to whittle it into a crutch. John helped the boy walk to their camp as Ben began to put together a noon meal with the sun high in the cloudy sky.

"Hungry?" Ben asked Whit.

"Some. I ain't et in two days."

"You spent the night in the mine?"

"Yeah. Them boys was plumb drunk when they come after me. Mean."

"Well, if they don't bother us," John said,

23

"we won't bother them."

"What about our cow?"

"Sometimes, it's best to take your losses and get up from the table," John said.

"What do you mean?"

"He means," Ben said, "you ain't goin' to get your milk cow back."

"Shoot," Whit said. "That ain't fair."

"Next time," John started to say, then thought better of it. "Well, don't let there be a next time."

"I got a gun," Whit said.

John looked up from the plate Ben handed him, and fixed the boy with a steely glint of his eyes.

"Guns cause more problems than they solve," he said. "Forget about packing iron."

"You both carry guns."

"I hate guns," John said softly.

Ben snorted.

John turned his head and glowered at Ben.

"Don't you say one damned word, Ben. Not one word."

Ben handed a plate of grub to Whit.

"I ain't sayin' a word," Ben said.

Whit took a fork and cut a new potato in half, sawed through a chunk of beef, and started eating.

Ben sat down and stared at the Colt on John's hip, the gun his father had modified for his son and left to him after his death.

"Sometimes, Ben," John said, "you can say a whole lot with your mouth shut."

Whit looked at the two men.

He had no idea what they were talking about, but he chewed his food thoughtfully in the ensuing silence.

All three were finishing up their lunch when John heard the slightest sound a few yards away. He set down his pewter plate and turned, cupping a hand to his right ear.

"You hear that, Ben?" he asked.

"What?"

Then, there it was again, the soft crunch of a boot on a dry tree branch, the crinkle of a loosened stone. Ben stopped chewing the last of the meat and stared in the direction John was looking.

John's right hand glided slowly toward the butt of his pistol.

That was as far as he got.

"You grab that hogleg and your brains will wind up on your plate, mister."

John stiffened and froze his hand in mid-air.

A burly man stepped out from behind a juniper, a rifle held level in his beefy scarred hands.

"Just nobody make any sudden moves," the man said, and two more men emerged from behind the trees. Each carried a rifle, and the first man cocked the hammer back.

Inside his head, John's mind ticked like a clock, a clock tied to a half dozen sticks of dynamite.

3

The three men all wore backpacks made out of heavy duck. The packs bristled with shovels, picks, pry bars, and chunks of milled wood. John saw the outlines of gold pans and tin cups as the men unslung the packs and dropped them on the ground. With their metal contents, the packs clanked like sacks of kitchen utensils.

John looked closely at the men, focusing on their eyes. The one who had spoken seemed to be their leader and the most dangerous. He had pale blue eyes and his gaze shifted from John to Whit, back and forth, as if trying to make a connection. He did not look at Ben much, which told John that the man did not consider the bearded old man much of a threat.

"You boys are a little bit off your range, ain't ye?" the bull-shouldered man said, looking directly at John Savage.

"Seems to me you're the ones who

drifted," John said, slowly and in an even, neutral tone of voice. "We're camped on our legal mining claim."

"We ain't seen no workings here. I'm claimin' this stretch of creek."

"I don't reckon you are," John said, fixing the man with a stare dark as night.

The man looked over at Whit, his eyes bulging with a hatred that was almost palpable.

"That kid there. He kin of yours?"

"Maybe," John said.

"You're a damned liar."

John didn't bat an eye. Instead, he let a slow smile flicker on his lips. It was almost like a leaf shadow, soft and subtle, as fleeting as if it had wings.

"You're good at name-calling," John said, in that soft even voice of his. "I wonder if you know anything about the bullets in my six-gun."

"Huh?"

The man's two friends stepped closer to their leader, menacing looks in their eyes. John noticed that their rifle barrels were pointed at the ground. They wouldn't open the ball, he was sure, and it would take them a second or two to aim their guns. Way too long for men who wanted to live past forty.

"My bullets have names," John said.

"Mister, I don't know what the hell you're talkin' about. Bullets don't have names."

"Mine do," John said.

The man shook his rifle as if it were a dust mop or a broom.

"You talk too damned much, mister," he said.

"I just thought you might want to know their names," John said.

"Makes no never-mind to me."

"One of my bullets is called Fate. Another is Destiny. In fact, three of them are named Fate and the other three are called Destiny."

"That makes about as much sense as you sayin' you got a claim here."

"Well, the ones called Fate are either warnings or a smashed leg. The Destiny bullets take out throats or brains. One smashes a man's heart to a bloody pulp."

While he was talking, John's hand had slid ever so slowly to the butt of his pistol.

"You shut your damned mouth or my rifle will do all the talkin'."

"We gonna shoot 'em all, Krieger?" The man closest to the bullish man spoke the words.

Krieger didn't answer. He started to bring his rifle up to his shoulder.

That was all John needed.

To everyone's surprise, John did two

things so fast, he caught the three strangers off guard for a split second. He got to his feet, but didn't stand up straight. Instead, he sidled to his right and drew his pistol so fast that it was a black blur in his hand. They all heard the snick of the cocking mechanism as John hammered back with his thumb. The pistol seemed to have a life of its own as he crouched, aimed, and fired with just a light squeeze of the hair-trigger.

Krieger screamed as the first bullet smashed into the stock of his rifle, right next to his hand. The stock splintered as the .45-caliber lead ball smashed into the wood, shredded it to sawdust. The rifle flew from Krieger's hands and bounced off a tree trunk and clattered to the ground. Before the other two could bring their rifles to bear, John swung his pistol and squeezed off two more shots. His bullets struck one man just above the kneecap, and he uttered a shrill cry of pain as his leg twisted under him and, off balance, he careened to the ground.

The third man jerked as the bullet ripped through his upper arm, close to the shoulder. His fingers went limp as he twisted into a human corkscrew and staggered backward. His hand opened involuntarily and the rifle slid from his grasp, struck the ground muzzle-first, stood upright for a half second, then fell over.

Smoke billowed from the muzzle of John's pistol, and he waded through it to stand over the three men, two of whom were clawing at their wounds. Krieger was on his knees, grasping his numb and stinging hand, a glazed look in his eyes.

All three men heard the pistol cock again. They all stared at the pistol's black snout as if it were a poisonous snake about to strike.

"There are three bullets left in the cylinder. Each one is named Destiny," John said. "Make your choice. You tasted a speck of Fate just now. Your destinies are waiting."

"God, man, don't shoot," Krieger said, his eyes wet and glittering.

"Don't shoot us," said the man squeezing his leg, blood pouring from a blue-black hole just above his kneecap, a splinter of bone poking through his fingers.

"No, man, you win," said the third man, his slitted eyes leaking tears as his wound painted his hand a bright red.

"You lose your rifles," John said, "and your sidearms. You walk back to your camp and never come down this creek again."

All three men nodded.

"I can't walk," the man with the wounded leg said.

"What's your name?" John asked, leveling

his pistol at him.

"Harry — Harry Short," the man stammered.

"And you?" The barrel of his pistol swung toward the man with a hole through his arm muscle.

"Peter Rosset," he said tightly, grimacing in pain. "Pete."

"And you, Krieger," John said. "You got a given name?"

"They call me Al," he said. "For Albert."

"I'll remember your names and your faces," John said. "Now, shuck those pistols and get on back up the creek before I change my mind."

The smell of burnt powder lingered in the still air as the three men lifted their pistols from their holsters and laid them on the ground. Krieger and Rosset helped Short to his feet. They made noise as they staggered through the leafy aspen branches, their boots crunching on rock and gravel. Soon, there was silence again, and John swung the cylinder out of his pistol, ejected the hulls, and slid three fresh cartridges into the empty chambers. The silver inlays on the pistol gleamed and sparkled in the sun as he turned to face Ben and Whit. The boy's eyes widened as he stared at the pistol, at the part of the barrel that bore a scripted legend in Spanish.

"Goshamighty," Whit said, "I never seen nothin' like that. What's that you got writ on your pistol, Mr. Savage?"

John stuck out his hand, let the boy read what it said.

"Is that Mexican?"

"Spanish, yes."

"What's it mean?"

Ben chuckled under his breath as he got to his feet. He walked over and began picking up the rifles and pistols that were strewn among the aspens.

"It means a great deal to me," said John. "My father gave this gun to me before he died. He modified it, gave it a hair-trigger, and had it engraved in silver."

"I wish I knew what it said." Whit watched as John pulled the pistol back and looked down at the barrel, the words.

"It says, *'No me saques sin razón, ni me guardes sin honor.'* "

"Huh?"

"It means, 'Do not draw me without reason, nor keep me without honor,' " John said.

"You had a reason to draw it, I reckon," Whit said.

John holstered the pistol. He didn't say anything right away.

33

He drew a breath, held it, then let the air out slowly.

"Sometimes," he said softly, "I think the pistol has a mind of its own."

Ben laid the weaponry down and looked long and hard at John as Whit's eyes shone with a faraway look of wonder.

"It's just a hunk of iron, John," Ben said. "It don't have no mind of its own."

John looked at Ben, his eyes narrowed. He could still feel the shock of the pistol's recoil in his hand, and the echoes of its booming voice still reverberated in his ears.

"It's more than that," he said, and turned away, walked down to the creek, squatted, and washed his hands in the cooling waters. He could still smell the acrid smoke, the burnt powder, and wondered if he would have killed those three men if they hadn't given up after his warning. He hadn't wanted to end their lives, but he had cocked his pistol a fourth time, and he could still feel the tingling in his trigger finger as it hovered near that delicate trigger, a hair breadth away from touching it.

He might have killed them.

The gun might have killed them. He thought he could still feel it pulsing in his hand, the grip throbbing against the muscles of his hand, as if it were breathing.

As if it were just waiting for that light touch of his finger to bring on its deadly roar, its lethal thunder.

He shook his head as if to throw away his thoughts, as if he could so easily dismiss them.

"Let's see about getting this boy back up to his home and his ma," he said to Ben. "After you hide those rifles and pistols real good."

"You show us the way, Whit," Ben said. "We'll get you home."

Whit said nothing. He was still looking at John Savage with something very close to awe.

4

Ben and John were slapping saddles on their horses when they heard a rustling in the aspens. They turned and saw Krieger, a wan, sheepish look on his face, pushing aside a low-hanging limb.

"Come back for our packs," he said, stooping to grab a strap on his own pack.

"Be quick about it," John said.

Krieger slung his own pack on his back and picked up the straps of the other two with his left hand. His right hand was red and swollen.

"Don't come back here," Ben said as Krieger turned away to walk back up the creek.

John shot a glance at Ben that was a dark scowl.

"Oh, you ain't seen the last of me," Krieger said, then turned to look at John. "What did you say your name was?"

"It's Savage. John Savage."

"I've heard that name before," Krieger said, his forehead furrowing in thought. "Yep, I sure as hell have."

"You might wish you never had," Ben said. "Now, git."

"I'm leavin', but you got some payback comin', Savage."

"If you want to keep breathing, Krieger, you'll forget about any payback."

Krieger grunted and walked off, rattling the aspen limbs, rustling the green leaves. His footsteps faded and it was quiet again as John pulled his cinch tight and buckled the strap.

"Some folks you just can't get shut of," Ben growled as he finished saddling Rusher.

John said nothing, but stared at the leaves of the aspens as they fluttered green and near white until they stopped moving.

"Whit, you ride double with Ben. You take us where you walked down to the creek. I'll follow."

Ben climbed into the saddle and reached for Whit's arm, pulled him up behind him.

"You ever rode a horse before?" Ben asked.

"Sure. Not one this big."

Ben chuckled. "Just wrap your arms around me and hold on," he said, then ticked his horse's flanks with his blunt

37

spurs. They rode downstream, John following, avoiding the talus debris at the base of the bluff. The creek made a slow bend and the bluff began to shrink until it finally disappeared for a good long stretch.

Whit pointed to a wide path next to another slight rise and Ben turned his horse.

"You been here before, ain't ye?" Whit said.

"Yep. Me'n John scouted that land up there many times whilst we was gold panning and blasting that mine of ours."

"We come up another way, but I found this path and come down it," Whit said.

"It's a old elk trail. Mule deer use it, too," Ben said.

"Yeah, I saw some old tracks. Lots of 'em."

Ben chuckled.

John rode up alongside the two and they all climbed up to the top together.

"John, what was all that about naming your bullets?" asked Ben. "I never heard you say that before."

"You keep a man's brain occupied, he's liable to let down his guard."

"Pretty slick. But how'd you know it would work?"

"I didn't, Ben. I just thought I'd give Krieger something to puzzle over while I got ready to take him down."

"Namin' bullets. I never thought of that."

"Krieger didn't, either," John said.

He took Gent over the top of the slight rise, and looked at acres of grass spread out for as far as he could see. Behind the vast meadow, the snowcapped peaks of the Rockies broke the skyline, their mantles gleaming white in the sun.

He waited for Ben and Whit to catch up to him, breathing deep of the thin air.

"Mighty pretty country," Ben said. "Just like I remembered it."

"We'll have cattle feeding on this grass pretty soon," John said.

"Yessir, we sure will."

"But you can't," Whit said. "Look yonder, up where the timber stands at the far end of this valley."

Ben and John looked where the boy was pointing.

"That your place?" Ben asked.

"It sure enough is."

Ben looked at John.

John shrugged and tapped Gent's flanks with his spurs.

"I don't see no cattle," Ben said.

"We ain't got none yet. Pa's gonna get us some and we're goin' to be rich. He's down in Denver now, buying us some breeding cattle."

Ben turned his head for a quick glance at John, but John's eyes remained fixed on the far mountains as if he were in some kind of trance.

And he was, for there was the fresh clean scent of dew-wet grass in the air, the perfume of wild columbines, pine, spruce, juniper, and fir, as heady as any fine brandy in a snifter. The grandeur of the land and the sheltered valley spread out before him, inducing a rapture that was mesmerizing. He could never get enough of it, and since he and Ben had first seen that pristine valley, he had wanted to live there, not on the land, but in it, surrounded by ancient mountains and trees thick as deep pile carpeting.

"Let's get the boy to home," John said, shaking his head slightly as if to free it of lofty thoughts and the nagging notion that squatters had ruined his dream by building a house on land he and Ben owned.

Grass grew on the tabletop, young sprouts no more than a few inches high, and the heady scent of small yellow flowers and budding columbines mingled with the scent of grass wafted on the vapors of evaporating dew. High clouds over the distant mountain peaks proclaimed a bright spring morning against an ocean-blue sky.

"I don't see any of our stakes," John said to Ben.

"Yeah, I noticed that."

"Did those stakes have numbers painted on 'em?" Whit said.

"They did," Ben said.

"I pulled 'em up. Pa gave me a penny for ever' one I carried back up to our camp. He used them for kindling."

"Damn, boy," Ben said, the rasp of irritation in his voice, "them stakes was markers for me and John's land boundaries. A hunnert and sixty acres apiece and we laid 'em out so's we have this whole wide valley to graze our cattle on."

"Pa said —"

"I don't give a damn what your pa said," John cut in. "You had no business pulling our stakes."

"I didn't know," Whit said with a sheepish whine. "Pa said —"

"Your pa said a hell of a lot," Ben said.

"Let's get this boy back home," John said, and Gent stepped out at his spurred urging.

John and Ben both knew where they had driven the stakes according to the land surveyor's instructions. The cabin lay square on one edge of their combined properties. John wanted to help the boy, but he knew he and Ben faced more than a homecom-

41

ing. The log cabin loomed as an intrusive force on land they had staked out, filed claims on, and in truth owned. The cabin spelled trouble, yet he wondered if he could throw the squatters off their land without a terrible tug at his conscience.

A man stepped out of the trees as Ben, John, and Whit rode up. He held an ax in his hands. He was sturdily built, a bronze cast to the face that peered out from under his sombrero, brown arms and hands, a red bandanna around his neck.

"Who's that?" Ben looked at Whit.

"That's Manolo Pacheco. We call him Manny. He works for us."

John held up his right hand, palm facing Manny Pacheco. Pacheco smiled and let the ax fall to the ground. He turned to the doorway of the house and spoke some words John couldn't hear. A moment later, a woman came to the open door, shaded her eyes with the flat of her right hand.

"Whit, is that you?" she called.

Whit waved at her.

A sign of relief flooded the woman's face as her hand fell away and sunlight washed across her features. She started to run toward her son.

Pacheco grinned and waved at Whit.

"Whit, I was so worried," the woman said

as Whit eased himself down, favoring his injured leg. The two embraced.

John looked at the woman's beaming face. She appeared to be in her late twenties, perhaps touching on thirty, with intense blue eyes, auburn hair, and finely chiseled features, a patrician nose, a dimpled chin. She gazed up at John, a look of silent gratitude in her eyes.

She looked somewhat regal in her faded gingham dress and her high-topped, lace-up boots, and it was difficult for John to picture this woman with a man like Argus Blanchett. The two did not seem suited to each other. Not at all.

"Ma'am," John said, doffing his hat. "You better keep this boy to home. He had a close call down on the creek."

"Whit's not tied to my apron strings, mister," the woman retorted. "What happened down at the creek?"

"Your boy can best tell you that, ma'am," John said. "May I light down?"

She appeared flustered for a moment, her eyes darting from side to side, her mouth opening in surprise, her hand flying to her hair to pat it down as if she were about to answer a knock on the door and wasn't expecting guests.

"Why, yes," she said, "how inconsiderate

of me. I thank you for bringing Whit home. Will you have some tea with us, fresh brewed, or I can make coffee."

Ben swung out of the saddle.

"Tea would be fine," John said, stretching a leg out to touch the ground as he held on to the saddle horn.

"Manny, tie their horses to the hitchin' post," the woman said.

"I'm John Savage, ma'am, and this is my partner, Ben Russell."

The woman held on to her son as she turned to go into the cabin.

"I'm sorry," she said. "I'm Emmalene Blanchett. Everyone calls me Emma."

"Ma'am," Ben said, tipping his hat courteously.

Before she reached the open door of the cabin, Emma called out.

"Eva."

John heard the scurry of feet inside the dwelling, and a second or two later, a young woman appeared in the doorway. John felt the air leave his lungs as if he had gasped aloud. She had long dark hair woven into twin pigtails that drooped over her small, comely shoulders. Her face was radiant and young, and her eyes were the blue of a mountain lake, vibrant and penetrating. They seemed to stare directly into his, and

44

he felt a shiver up his spine as if he were standing under a trickling waterfall and ice-cold water was dripping on the back of his neck.

"Eva, get out the cups and pour tea for all of us."

She turned to John, who gaped at Eva like a poleaxed imbecile, his mouth wide open, his eyes enlarged to the size of agates.

"That's my daughter Evangeline," she said. "We call her Eva."

"Yes'm," John muttered as Eva disappeared and Emma stepped up into the cabin. He stood there, frozen to the spot where he had halted.

Ben slapped him between the shoulder blades.

"You just goin' to stand there, Johnny, gawkin' like a love-struck schoolboy?"

"Aw, shut up, Ben. She's just a girl." His voice was pitched low and it was soft as eiderdown, but Ben heard him. He heard the croak and the husk in John's voice, and saw the light dancing in the man's eyes for just the shaved fraction of a second. But he knew his friend was smitten, and he knew how hard the road ahead was going to be, not only for John Savage, but for Emma, Eva, Whit, and himself as well.

But Ben said nothing.

He just wondered how and when John was going to tell this family that he had killed Argus Blanchett, husband and father, less than ten days ago in Cherry Creek.

He followed John into the dark cabin, and it was like stepping into a funeral parlor in some small poor desolate town.

5

Al Krieger glared at Pete Rosset and Harry Short. Harry was wrapping gauze around his calf and Pete was daubing an aromatic salve on his arm, wincing with each touch, tears eking from his eyes as he gritted his teeth to bite off the pain.

"You sorry bastards," Krieger said.

"What the hell happened?" another man said as he walked up from the creek, his shoes dripping with every step, his pants legs soaked to the knees. He was carrying a bucket and the water was sloshing over the rim, splotching the ground.

"Gimme that bucket, Corny," Krieger said, holding out his left hand.

Dave Cornwall slipped the rope handle into Krieger's hand.

"I was goin' to make some coffee with that," Corny said.

Krieger set the bucket down and plunged his right hand into the water. He squatted, then sat down, letting his hand float in the cool water.

"You can have it back when I'm done."

"What's wrong with your hand?" Corny asked.

Harry snickered.

"Huh?" Corny said, an inane expression on his face.

"You shoulda been with us," Pete said. "We found that kid."

"The kid busted your hand, Al? The kid we stole the cow from? That cow's over there, tethered to a tree."

"No, the damned kid didn't bust my hand."

"Where are your rifles?"

Pete bent his head to point downstream.

"You left 'em down at the new place you was goin' to try?" Corny said.

"Yeah," Harry said. "We just left them down there for seed."

"For seed?"

"You know, to grow more rifles."

"Aw," Corny said, a sheepish grin cracking open his face. "You're funnin' me."

"No, we ain't Corny," Pete said. "We forgot our rifles. Al wants you to go down there and bring 'em back to us."

"Well, why didn't you say so?" Corny said, and started walking through the littered camp with its four small tents and one large one for their supplies of picks, shovels, rockers, foodstuffs, medicines, ropes, horse blankets, saddles, bridles, and other tack.

Al glared at the young man and shook his head.

"Corny, come on back," he said. "Pete's full of shit. We run into trouble downstream. Got shot at. You start packin' your pistol and keep a rifle handy. Those jaspers just might ride up here and try to snuff our lamps."

"Aw, Al . . ."

"He's not kidding, Corny," Harry said. "You start packin' iron and dig out those extra rifles for us. Man, I never saw such shootin'."

"Who shot you?" Corny asked as he walked toward the supply tent, stumbling over an empty airtight that had once contained peaches.

"Some bastard what says he's already got that stretch of creek we wanted to prospect," Al said, moving his hand up and down in the bucket.

"He was some slick, Corny," Harry said. "Had a fancy pistol, and was faster'n a snake."

"Yeah," Pete said, "that hogleg fairly shone with silver inlays."

"Inlays?"

"Like some kind of writing, I reckon. I only got a quick peek at it. Sun hit that silver and made it shine like lightning."

"You boys were too slow," Krieger said. "One of you should have dropped him when he shot my rifle out of my hand."

"Al, that corker didn't give us time to think," Harry said.

"You can't even think slow, Harry," Krieger said.

"Well, he caught you first, Al. You always brag about how fast you can draw and shoot."

"He didn't give no warning," Pete said. "No warning at all."

"I bet I could take him," Corny said.

"Well, you just go on down there and brace that bastard, Corny, and bring our rifles back."

Corny's face blanched as if he'd been punched in the stomach. He looked down at the glistening creek. Lights danced in its mottled waters and he had to squint out the glare. He pulled in a breath and turned to Harry.

"How fast was he?"

"You never saw a man so fast, Corny. He was like a rattlesnake."

"I'll get him," Krieger said. "One day I'll

50

get that bastard."

"Maybe you ought to wait until Thatcher and Ferguson get back from Denver, Al," Corny said. "Then we could all go down there and give him what for."

"Thatcher's due back any time," Pete said, looking off to the east. Nothing but trees, but he knew where Denver lay.

"Probably today, I reckon," Harry said, tying a knot in his bandage.

"Thatcher will know what to do, all right," Pete said, adjusting his injured arm inside his shirt, between two buttons. A makeshift sling.

"Yeah, Lem Thatcher's just as fast as that jasper," Harry said. "Maybe faster, I think."

"We won't catch that man off guard again," Krieger said. "There was something in his eyes." He paused, lifted his hand out of the water, and let it drip as it hung there above the bucket. "Something unholy."

"You mean a devil," Corny said.

"I mean seven kinds of devil."

"I say leave him alone," Harry said, sitting down on a flat rock. The rock teetered under his buttocks and he lifted one cheek, slid the rock an inch to the side, and it steadied. "What the hell do we need his digs for, anyway?"

"You're so damned dumb, Harry," Krieger

said. "Haven't you figured it out yet?"

"Figured out what?"

Krieger raised his arm and pointed downstream with his left hand.

"See all them riffles? Just below our claims. Well, the creek makes a run there and drops off maybe a foot or two beyond it, then hurries like a sumbitch right where those guys have their claim. There's probably a mother lode somewhere near here, underground or up in them rocks. All the dust and nuggets are washing down on their claim while we're lucky to pan out five or ten bucks a day."

"You figure that, do you, Al?"

"Damned right I do. And I'll bet Thatcher will see it that way, too. We ain't been here a month and I been studying that creek. It's taking from us and giving to that gunslick down there."

"Shit," Corny said.

"Shit is right," Pete said. "That sure looked like a good stretch of creek down there. Water rushin' past a good long stretch, diggin' out high banks. Them boys got them a payin' claim and we got nothin' here but back-breakin' work."

Only Corny did any panning, while the other three men lolled in the shade. The sun reached its zenith, and then began the slow descent toward the high, snowcapped peaks to the west. It was mid-afternoon when Walt Ferguson and Lemuel Thatcher rode into camp, their clothes and faces soaked with sweat, their boots dulled by dust. Their horses' hides were streaked. The pack mule, lugging a full pannier of supplies, clomped into the creek after them and came to a dead stop in the middle of it.

Lem rode behind the mule and whacked its rump until it jumped to the opposite bank.

"Corny the only one workin'?" Thatcher said, glaring at Krieger.

"We got us a tale to tell, Lem," Krieger said.

Thatcher swung out of the saddle, the stub of a cigar between his teeth, a scowl chiseling his lean face.

"Well, I got a few tales to tell myself, Krieger. What's goin' on here? What's wrong with your hand?"

"It's a long story," Krieger said as Ferguson dismounted and slipped the mule's rope over the saddle.

Ferguson took off his hat, revealing a shock of blond hair. He wiped his forehead and the sweatband, then put his hat back on and led the mule to a small aspen and wrapped the rope around the tree, tied it off

53

in a series of three knots.

"Playin' grab-ass, Al?"

"Nope, me and them two, Pete and Harry, run into some trouble this morning."

"Not much trouble you can get into when you're pannin' for gold, Krieger."

"We went down past the rapids to do some pannin'," Krieger said. "Thought it was unclaimed. Feller there drew down on us and sent lead a-flyin'. I got my rifle knocked out of my hand and the others caught slugs. The man was fast. Mighty fast."

Thatcher looked at Pete and Harry, crunched down on his cigar, shifted it to the other side of his mouth. Ferguson untied the ropes on the canvas covering the pannier and let it all drop to the ground. He began stacking foodstuffs atop the tarp, taking in every word, but not looking at anyone.

"This feller have a name?" Thatcher said.

"I think his name was John something," Harry said.

"Savage. It was John Savage," Pete said.

Thatcher's mouth opened and the cigar fell out. He caught it in his hand, but his mouth stayed open, widened as his jaw dropped another half inch.

Ferguson stopped unloading the pannier

and turned around, his face drained of color, his eyes squinted to a pair of dark slits.

"Jesus," Ferguson said.

Thatcher stuck the cigar stub back in his mouth, bit down on it.

"Have himself a pistol all shiny with silver inlays?"

"Yeah," Krieger said. Pete and Harry both nodded, sheepish looks on their faces.

"You're lucky, Al," Thatcher said. "Me'n Fergie saw him put a man's lights out so quick, we had to look twice to believe it."

Krieger's Adam's apple bobbed against his throat as he swallowed hard.

Ferguson walked over, forsaking his chore of unloading the goods they had bought down in Denver.

"Al," he said, "you're one dumb sonofabitch."

Thatcher's mouth twisted in a wry smile.

"How come?" Krieger asked, blinking both eyes in bewilderment.

"You ever hear of Ollie Hobart?"

"I heard something about him, I reckon. Had a gang, was some kind of highwayman."

"He wasn't no highwayman, Al," Thatcher said. "He was a claim jumper and he robbed some miners a couple of years back. Killed 'em all."

"Except two," Ferguson said. "He missed an old geezer named Ben Russell and a young'un named John Savage. Hobart kilt Savage's ma and pa and his little sister. Ever hear about that?"

"No, I reckon not. I thought Hobart was dead."

"He is dead," Ferguson said. "And all of his bunch. Ever' damned one of 'em kilt by John Savage and Ben Russell. Two men against a whole gang."

"Christ," Al breathed, his face pale as a winter sunrise.

"And we saw Savage down at Cherry Creek. He killed a man named Argus Blanchett in a fair fight. Fair for him, not Argus."

Thatcher took in a deep breath, pulled the cigar from his mouth.

"I wondered where Savage's claim was," he said. "Now, I know, and it don't make me feel real good."

Krieger moved the muscles in his face, scrunching it up as he opened and closed his eyes.

"I don't feel real good, neither," he said.

"Corny," Ferguson said, "you start totin' them goods to the supply tent." He walked back to the mule and started throwing airtights to the ground, dropping sacks of flour and beans in a heap.

"Cool down, Fergie," Thatcher said.

"Damn Krieger, anyway. Now we got trouble 'cause of him."

"And we've got a worthless claim on this stretch of creek," Thatcher said. He spit out the wet wad that was left of his cigar, and turned to face Ferguson. "Maybe we can put our heads together and come up with something that might work for us."

"Like what?" Ferguson said.

"Like make a silk purse out of a sow's ear," Thatcher said, an enigmatic smile on his face. "Maybe it's time Savage's clock run down."

"Hobart probably thought the same thing a time or two," Ferguson said. "And he had a dozen men or more."

"Hobart might have had too many men. Made him careless. It would take only one man to kill Savage. One man against another."

"Jesus," Ferguson said again.

"That part of a prayer, Fergie," Thatcher said, "or the start of a curse?"

6

When John sat down at the table opposite Emma, he took a good look at her. Sunlight streamed through the window and lit her face. He saw the dark blotches on her cheekbones, the faint smudges along the jawline, and one on her throat. Eva was rattling tin and porcelain in the small kitchen, and the Mexican was still standing in the doorway. Ben was scooting out his chair, and Emma seemed nervous and ill at ease.

"I'm so glad you brought my son back to me," she said, looking directly into John's eyes.

John cleared his throat and shifted his glance to Whit, who sat down on a polished stump that served as a makeshift chair. He sat in front of a small fireplace with a smoke-blackened hearth, half-burned logs in the fireplace, a mantel decorated with small mountain stones. The entire cabin reeked of poverty and hardship, but the smell of brewing tea and bread baking in the oven spoke of warmth and friendship, of a family making do on next to nothing.

Eva walked up to the table carrying a small tin tray laden with cups and a chipped porcelain teapot. She set the cups and teapot down and sat in a nearby chair.

"Aren't you having tea, Eva?" her mother said.

"No'm. I'll just sit."

Emma poured tea into the cups and smiled wanly at John, as if trying to express her gratitude at his returning her son to her.

"I just can't thank you enough, sir," she said, filling her cup last. "Eva and I were so worried. All night. I couldn't sleep and Eva was crying. We just didn't know what to do and we didn't know what had happened to Whit."

John blew on the steaming tea and took a sip, set his cup down on the pine table.

"Ma'am, I'm afraid I didn't bring Whit back up here just out of the kindness of my heart."

Ben stiffened as he sipped his hot tea.

"Oh?"

"No, ma'am. After Ben and I talked to him, and found out where he lived, I was plumb curious."

"Curious? About what?"

"About who was living on my land," he said, and waited for the shock to take effect on Emmalene Blanchett.

She took it better than he would have thought. She was momentarily speechless, but recovered quickly.

"Just what do you mean, sir?"

"Well, Ben and I filed homestead papers on three hundred and twenty acres here and have plans to raise cattle up here. You built right on one corner of my land."

"Why, that's just not possible. My husband . . ."

"Do you have papers?" John asked. "Maybe he got his survey figures mixed up."

"Pa didn't file no papers before we come here," Whit said. "He's down in Denver taking care of that. He should be back up here any day."

"That's right," Emma said.

"He surveyed the land up here? Didn't he see our stakes?"

Emma shook her head. "I — I don't know." She looked over at Manolo Pacheco, who shrugged and rolled his eyes back in their sockets.

"Look, ma'am," John said.

"Will you please call me Emma? And how may I address you and your friend?"

"I'm John Savage and this is Ben Russell."

"Pleased to meet you both," she said, a timid squeak in her tone.

"Ma'am, I'm not going to boot you and your family off my land. I just want you to know that I own it. There's plenty of land right around us and I can help you to homestead it. We could be neighbors, if you like."

"Well, I don't know. I'll have to talk to Argus about it when he gets back. I'm sure he can straighten all this out to your satisfaction, John."

John took another sip of tea, looked down at the table. He knew Ben was staring at him, wondering how he was going to squirm out of the deep hole he was digging for himself.

He heard Ben clear his throat, and knew it was forced.

Eva walked to the table and stood behind her mother, looking at John Savage. He looked up at her and their eyes met. He felt something melt inside him, some liquid filling his heart, searing it with a lava heat. He felt his stomach twist up and try to tie itself in a knot. He looked back down at Emma, looked into her eyes. They were innocent of all knowledge, but Eva suspected something. When she had heard her father's name, she had come to stand behind her mother immediately. As if to protect her.

"Ma'am, is your husband Argus Blanchett?"

"Why, yes, that's his full name. Do you know him?"

Ben scooted his chair back an inch or so from the table. The scraping sound filled the silent room.

"No, ma'am, I don't know him. Didn't, I mean."

"Didn't?"

John steeled himself to tell her the truth about her husband. At the same time, he looked over at Whit and turned his head to mark where Pacheco was standing. He had to know where everyone was in case the boy and the Mexican tried to jump him.

"Your husband, ma'am, is buried down in Cherry Creek. He's not coming back. I'm sorry."

There was a deeper silence in the room now. A stunned silence. And, as John glanced at all those present, they seemed frozen in time, frozen like figures in a museum.

Emma did not cry. He had expected her to break down and begin wailing like a grieving wife.

Instead, Eva put both hands on her mother's shoulders and squeezed her gently. John looked up at Eva and saw that her face was immobile, without expression, her soft blue eyes slightly dulled, either from shadow or from a terrible grief. And then, as he looked at her, her eyes widened and they glistened like blue sapphires, as if they were smiling while her face remained rigid.

"Argus . . . dead?" Emma said.

"Yes'm, I'm afraid so," John said.

"How did he die?" she said tightly.

Ben squirmed in his seat. His right hand dropped to the butt of his pistol, as if it was an old habit of his.

"He was shot," John said, his voice pitched low, soft and smooth as flowing honey.

"Shot? Who shot him?"

"I did, ma'am," John said. "I shot him."

"You killed my . . . you killed Argus?"

Disbelief crawled across Emma's face. The muscles in her cheekbones twitched involuntarily. Her lips and chin quivered as if she had been struck a hard blow across her face.

"It was self-defense," Ben blurted out. "Argus pulled a gun on John."

Everyone in the room looked at Ben. Emma's eyes narrowed with suspicion.

"I swear," Ben said, but he kept his hand on the butt of his pistol.

"Is that true, Mr. Savage?" Emma said,

shifting her attention back to John.

"Yes'm, your husband did draw down on me."

"Why?"

"Ma'am, I don't think you want to know all of it right now. Maybe later when you've cried out your grief and accepted your husband's death."

Emma stiffened in her chair. She sat up, her back straight, her blue eyes clear, her jaw firmly set.

Out of the corner of his eye, John saw Pacheco cross himself with quick movements of his right hand. His lips moved as he invoked the names of the Trinity in Spanish. There would be no threat from there, he thought.

He glanced over at Whit, wondering if the boy would jump off the stump and rush him, blinded by fury over the death of his father. Whit had a quizzical look on his face, an almost rapturous look, and the faintest trace of a little crooked smile. Or was John just imagining that the boy was starting to smile, that he was not mad or suffering from grief?

Whit just sat there, stunned, and then he closed his eyes and John thought he was going to cry. When the young man opened his eyes again, they were dry and clear, and he looked at John as though the man who had killed his father was to be praised, or worshipped.

"I do want to know," Emma said, and touched a finger to one of the bruises on her face. "I want to know what Argus was doing that you had to shoot him."

"Ma'am . . ." John said, shaking his head.

"Go on, Johnny," Ben said. "Tell her the whole thing. You got nothin' to be ashamed of."

"Is that true, Mr. Savage?" Emma said. "You're not ashamed that you killed my husband?"

John let her words wash through him and soak into him. Ashamed was the wrong word, he thought. There was nothing to be ashamed of in the killing of Argus Blanchett. The man was an animal, a vicious, cruel, lustful sonofabitch. But he couldn't tell his widow that, especially not in front of her children, who must be filled with hatred toward their father's killer.

"I'm not ashamed, exactly," John said. "The man brought it on himself. I didn't like killing him. I don't like killing anyone. But he was going to kill me, and if I hadn't called him out . . ."

"You called him out?" Emma leaned forward over the table. Her daughter's

65

hands slipped from her shoulders.

"Ma'am, he was trying to put the boots to a young girl. A girl he was beating with his fists until her face was a bloody pulp."

He saw Eva shudder and Emma stiffened again, sat straight and rigid as if she had received a shock of electricity up her spine.

The room went dead silent again. The silence was as thick as a feather quilt, heavy, stifling, breathless.

"What do you mean, 'trying to put the boots to her'? Was he trying to kill her?"

"No ma'am. He was . . ."

John couldn't say it. He looked at Ben and let out a long breath.

"What he's tryin' to say, ma'am," Ben said, "was that this Argus feller, ah, I mean your husband, had torn off all the girl's clothes and stripped his own trousers off. He was on top of that young girl and trying to deflower her. It was downright brutal, ma'am."

Emma gasped and leaned backward in her chair as if a strong wind had gusted inside the room and pinned her to the back of her chair. Eva's eyes closed tightly like a pair of tiny fists, and she brought her hands up to her mouth as if to stifle a scream.

Whit stood up, his eyes wild, rolling in all

directions like steel balls that had been magnetized.

"You mean he was trying to rape her," he said, and then clenched his fists and began to shake all over.

John didn't answer him, although Whit was looking straight at him.

"He was dang sure rapin' that pretty young gal," Ben said. "Nobody stopped him 'ceptin' John here, who told Argus to back off. Argus grabbed up his pistol and aimed it straight at John. He got the hammer pulled back. John drew his own pistol real fast and put . . . well, he shot Argus and he fell back dead as a stone. Sorry, ma'am, but that's the way it was. John helped the gal up and took off his shirt, give it to her, and got her out of there, back to her wagon."

"Is that what happened, Mr. Savage?" Emma asked, her voice calm, level, and without rancor.

"I reckon. Ben saw it. I was in the middle of it."

"Have you killed many men in your life?"

"Yes. I have."

"Are you a gunman, then, Mr. Savage?"

"I don't call myself a gunman. No, ma'am."

"You sound like one. You look like one."

"I'm really sorry, ma'am. If there was any

other way to . . ."

"Don't apologize," she said. "You did what you had to do. I — I guess there's nothing left for me. I'm on your property and as soon as we can, we'll go down to Denver and try to make a life for ourselves."

"Ma, no," Eva said. "I don't want to leave here. He said we could stay, didn't you, mister?"

John looked at Eva. She was a beautiful young woman and there was a pleading in her blue eyes. He felt the tug of her, the urgency in her voice.

"Yes, I did. You all can stay here. Maybe you can help Ben and me and we can put money in your purse." There was a silence again, and this time it was laden with palpable tension. John could feel it. He thought he knew what Emma was thinking. How could she work for a man who had killed her husband?

How could she even look at him without thinking of what he had done?

His pistol felt heavy on his belt just then. It felt as if it was made of pure lead and something was pushing it against his leg until his skin caught fire.

7

John was not prepared for what happened next. Eva walked over to him and leaned down, kissed him on the cheek. He felt that small strip of flesh on his face turn hot and spread wide in a blushing stain. He touched the spot and looked up at her.

"That was to show my gratitude," Eva said.

Her mother's eyes widened in shock and she frowned in disapproval.

"Eva, where are your manners? Your respect for your father?"

Eva's eyes sparked with a sudden flare of rage and she wheeled to face her mother.

"Respect for my father?" she said. "What he was doing to that poor girl was what he was trying to do with me, Ma. I'm glad he's dead. I'm glad he won't come sneakin' around at night when I'm in bed. I'm glad —"

Emma rose from her chair, walked over to

her daughter, and slapped Eva across the face. Eva's neck bent from the force of the blow and she looked as if she would fall down. John half rose from his chair and put his arm around Eva's waist, holding her.

"That's enough," Emma said, her voice low and controlled, the words slipping through tight lips. "I won't have you profane a dead man, my husband and your own father. Do you hear?"

Whit got up and John turned to him, stuck out his arm with his hand open to stop the young man from getting into the thick of the mother-daughter squabble.

"Look what he did to you, Ma," Whit said, stopping in his tracks. "He beat you. He beat all of us."

"You keep your mouth shut, Whit," Emma said. "I won't have you talking that way in front of strangers."

"Aw, Ma, why don't you face up to it? You're glad Pa's dead, too."

Emma's eyes blazed, narrowed to slits. Her lips compressed until they were bloodless. She took in a deep breath, held it, held it like the rage that was building inside her. She closed her eyes and squeezed them so tight, John thought they would never open again.

"Ma'am," he said. "Emmalene. Just calm

down, won't you?"

Emma opened her eyes.

"I think you've worn out your welcome here, John Savage," she said. "Go back to where you came from. I never want to see you again."

John let his arm slip away from Eva's waist. He stepped back from the table.

Eva stared at him, a desperate look in her eyes.

"Ma, don't," she said, and John saw a tenderness in the young woman's eyes that was like a soft hand squeezing his heart.

Emma glared at John, but her gaze softened as Eva guided her mother back to her chair and sat her down. Emma said nothing for a few seconds as she studied John's face, as if she were trying to decide what kind of man he was.

"Mr. Savage," she said, "I don't know what to think of you. You have killed a man. My husband. You say that you had to kill him. That if you had not shot him, he would have killed you. How can you be sure? Was there no other way?"

"No, ma'am, there wasn't. As Ben told you, he had his pistol aimed straight at me and he was cocking the hammer back."

"Yet, you . . . you shot him first."

"John's very fast, ma'am," Ben said. "The

fastest man with a gun I've ever seen."

"How did he get that way, Mr. Russell? By shooting and killing other men?"

"You don't have to answer that, Ben," John said. "It's a question for me. And maybe you have the right to ask it, Mrs. Blanchett. So, I'll answer."

"I wish you would," she said.

"We live in a dangerous world, ma'am. I saw my whole family slaughtered by vicious gunmen down on the creek below this valley. My mother, father, and little sister. They killed Ben's brother and many others that day. There is no law out here. The men stole our gold and rode on. Ben and I were spared because we were up in a mine shaft and had no weapons. My father left me a pistol which those men didn't take, and I used it to exact an eye for an eye. I didn't want to kill them, but they wanted to kill me. And Ben."

"You . . . you killed them all?" Emma gasped.

"Ben and I killed them all, yes. Each one was given the chance to surrender and go to trial. Instead, they tried to kill me."

"That sounds almost heartless," Emma said.

"Ma!" Eva said.

"It wasn't heartless, ma'am," John said. "I

72

did not like to have the power of life and
death over another man. I hated killing
those men. But they were bad men and they
would not listen to reason. I wish I could
hang up my gun and never fire it again."

"But you won't," she said.

"No, ma'am, I won't. This morning three
men tried to kill me, Ben, and Whit there.
They were claim jumpers from up the creek.
They beat the tar out of your son and they
wanted our claim for themselves."

"So, you killed them," Emma said.

John sighed and did not answer.

"No, ma'am," Ben said, "he didn't kill
them. They had the drop on us, three rifles
aimed at us. John could have killed them,
but he didn't. He gave them all fair warning
and when they were going to shoot us, he
drew his pistol."

"He didn't kill 'em, Ma," Whit said. "He
shot to wound them, and he took their rifles
away and sent them back up the creek like
dogs with their tails tucked between their
legs. He didn't kill 'em, Ma."

She looked at Whit, reading his face.

"I believe you, Whit," she said. "And I
believe Mr. Russell. I — I didn't know any
of this. Why didn't you kill them, Mr. Savage?"

"I don't honestly know. I'm tired of killing. It's a terrible thing to kill a man. But I think your husband would have killed me and I'm almost certain he would have killed that young gal, too. When he was finished with her, I mean."

"Pa might have, Ma," Eva said. "I mean, he might have killed that poor girl. You know he was capable of it."

Emma hung her head. Then she began to sob, quietly, softly.

"I'm sorry, Emma," John said. "Sorry to cause you such grief."

Eva drew a small kerchief from her pocket and began dabbing at her mother's cheeks. Emma lifted her head and took the handkerchief from Eva and made small semicircles under her eyes, wiping away the tears.

"Thank you for saying that, Mister . . . ah, John. It means a lot to me. Argus was a mean man. But he was my man, and I did love him at one time, and for some time after we were married. But after Whit was born and as Evangeline was growing into a young woman, he changed. He became cruel and demanding. Nothing suited him. Nothing about me, that is. I couldn't keep the house clean enough for him. I couldn't cook his meals good enough. He treated Whit like a slave, and paid too much attention to Eva. But I thought he would change after we came up here. I truly did.

"He went to Denver to get some cattle, said we could make a fresh start up here. We had a little money saved up, but Argus was fond of corn likker and I was worried he'd spend it all down in that sinful town. I never thought he'd . . . he'd do what you say he did."

John and Ben looked at each other, but neither said a word. Eva started to tear up, and Whit bowed his head and seemed to be shaking inside, whether from memories or grief, John couldn't be sure.

"People sometimes change, Emma," John said, and knew when he said it that it was too weak. Men like Argus Blanchett didn't change. They just became meaner and crueler as they got away with more and more. If no one stood up to such men, they just got worse.

"Can you tell me what that girl looked like, John?" Emma said.

John was surprised at the question.

"Was she pretty? Did she look like Eva?"

"I don't know," John said.

"She was pretty badly beaten, ma'am, but I saw her before your man got a holt of her," Ben said. "She was mighty purty, and I reckon she did bear some resemblance to your daughter, now that I think of it."

"Then, that explains it," Emma said. "Argus was obsessed with Eva, but I didn't know he lusted after her. I just thought he was, well, overly protective."

Eva's face changed expressions three or four times, and John could see that she was fighting her feelings. She looked like a trapped rabbit with half its foot sawed off, struggling and in pain.

"Now is not the time for you to pack up your family and leave the mountains, Emma," John said. "Feel that mountain breeze floating through the windows? Smell that fresh spring grass growing? There is perfume floating in here from the flowers. Deer and elk are bedded down in the cool shade of the pines and spruce. Partridges are fluffing their feathers in the dust. It's peaceful up here and the high peaks are your guardians, watching over you.

"In a few days, maybe a couple of weeks," he went on, "my drovers will come up here with three dozen head of whiteface cattle. They're going to build corrals, cabins, a barn. They'll need help, and I can pay you and your family in gold or greenbacks, provide you with food. You're not only welcome to stay, but I want you to stay. I'm trying to build a small ranch here, something to rely on when the gold in the creek runs out. Give it a try, Emma."

"Can we stay, Ma?" Eva pleaded. "Please, oh, please."

"Ma, I want to stay, too," said Whit. "Ben and John are good friends."

Emma looked over at Pacheco, who had not said a word.

"Manolo? What do you think?"

Pacheco walked over to the table and stood next to John.

"You would hire me?" he said.

"Yes. My drovers are Mexicans. You would be able to speak the tongue."

"I have no place to go," Pacheco said. "I have no family. I will stay, but not because you hire me, Mr. Savage. I stay because I have heard of you and I have heard of the gun you carry."

Emma's face brightened with surprise.

"Manolo, you have heard of this man?"

"Oh, yes. We have heard of how his family was killed and how he and his friend, Mr. Ben, tracked them down. And his gun, his *pistola*, that is very famous, too. Because there is something written on it that every-one in my country and all the *mejicanos* know, and we believe that Mr. Savage honors what is written on his six-gun."

"May I see your pistol, John?" Emma said.

"I don't know," John said. "I don't show it

off much."

"I want to see it, too," Eva said.

"I've seen it," Whit said. "It's a beauty."

John drew his pistol, his hand moving slow. He laid it on the table next to his cup. The sunlight glanced off the silver legend engraved on the barrel.

Emma and Eva walked over and bent down to look at it. Whit came over, too, and stood there, a smug look of satisfaction on his face.

"What does it say, Manolo?" Emma asked.

"It says, *'No me saques sin razón, ni me guardes sin honor.'* That is what it says."

Emma shook her head and looked at John.

"What does it mean?"

"Manolo can tell you, Emma," John said.

"It says, 'Do not draw me without reason, nor keep me without honor.' That is what it means in English."

"Why, that's beautiful, John."

"My father meant it when he engraved those words on the barrel," John said.

"My *compadres* call it *la pistola salvaje,*" Pacheco said. "The gringos call it the Savage Gun. They said it has much power."

Emma let out a long sigh. She looked at Whit and then at Eva. Her eyes softened and sparkled with leftover tears.

"We will stay, John Savage. I thank you

78

for your kind offer. Now put that gun away before I faint."

Everyone laughed.

But John holstered the pistol just before Emma wrapped her arms around him and hugged him close for just a fraction of a second.

That was enough. John felt her energy and knew that he had made a friend of a very strong woman.

8

Ben was not a man to hide his grumpiness. On the ride back down to the creek, he let John have it with both barrels.

"I ain't goin' to nursemaid no kid who's still wet behind the ears, John."

"No, you're not going to nursemaid Whit," John said. "You're going to teach him to build dry rockers, sluice boxes, and how to pan that creek for gold."

"Big mistake hirin' those folks back there. 'Specially that kid."

"Whit's not much younger than I was when we all came up here, Ben."

"He's not half as smart."

"We're all dumb about some things until someone teaches us. He'll learn."

"And that Mex and them wimmin'. Holy Jehosephat, John, you're buyin' into nothin' but trouble. I would have sent the whole bunch packin'."

"Grumble, grumble, grumble," John said.

"I ain't grumblin', I just think we got enough on our plates 'thout takin' on a family what can't rub two nickels together."

"We're going to need hands once we get cattle up here. You just don't look far enough ahead, Ben."

"Well, I ain't payin' them nothin' out of my poke."

The wind that was sleeping in the high country awakened and blew down on their backs, drying the sweat on their shirts. It carried the tang of snow in its teeth, and gathered the scent of wildflowers and young grasses, the fragrances of pines, spruce, and juniper. The high fluffy clouds blew across the blue sky like sailing ships, and pulled shadows across the trail in blue-gray smudges from the ghostly hand of an invisible painter. The land seemed to shift and rise through sunlight and shadow tilting under them like a restless sea.

"Is that the way it's going to be, Ben? You living on your homestead, me on mine?"

"I didn't mean no such thing, Johnny. I just don't want the responsibility of that orphaned family. You killed Argus Blanchett, not me."

"Would you have killed him if you were in my shoes, Ben?"

Ben worried that bone over in his mind

81

for several seconds.

"I reckon. But I didn't. It's your guilt you have to live with. I don't have none."

"Not your brother's keeper, eh?"

"I didn't mean it that way, neither. I just think we ought to have got shut of them folks soon as we brought Whit back to 'em. We got enough to do, what with cattle comin' up and them claim jumpers breathin' down our necks."

"I'll take on that worry, too, Ben. You just crawl into your little hole and shrivel up like a prune. Don't worry about a blamed thing."

"If that's the way you want it, Johnny boy."

The men rode in silence the rest of the way to their camp on the creek. Ben was sullen the rest of the day, until Whit rode down on a swaybacked old bay mare he called Rosie. Her moth-eaten hide was covered with dried scabs and fresh deer fly bites that ran red down her sides and legs.

"That horse won't last the winter, boy," Ben said as Whit dismounted.

"She ain't but nine or ten years old."

"And way past pasturing. You keep her separate from our horses, boy. Take her yonder over the creek and hide her behind them aspen."

"My name's Whit, not boy."

"Until you get some starch in your britches, sonny, you ain't got no name with me."

Whit looked over at John, who shrugged his shoulders until his neck disappeared.

"You'll have to make your own way here, Whit," John said. "Ben's got his ways."

"I'm mighty glad you asked me to work for you, Mr. Savage."

"Call me John. There are no misters here. Can you saw wood? Handle hammer and nail?"

"I reckon so. I helped Manolo build our cabin, nailed the winder and door frames, sawed 'em up, too."

"Get your horse taken care of and help Ben. He'll teach you a few things."

"Like hell," Ben gruffed, but he walked to the supply tent and started laying out lumber to build a dry rocker.

"You want me to ride Rosie to the other side of the creek?" Whit asked John.

"Yes, but go through the shallows right here. See those big rocks down below us, sticking up out of the water?"

"Yes."

"Stay away from that stretch of creek. It's a deep hole for a long stretch and those rocks and the rushing water make a whirlpool that will suck you down and drown you. We lost a mule in that hole. For all I know the mule's still down there. Its bones, anyway."

"I won't go nowheres near it," Whit said. He rode across the creek a few moments later and waded back after he had hobbled Rosie in a grassy glade. The breeze from the mountains stiffened as the day wore on.

While Ben was showing Whit how to make a dry rocker, John carried bedrolls and foodstuffs up to the mine. He laid out three beds. Then he made two beds near the fire ring next to the creek. As the sun was falling toward the distant snowcaps, he dug out a pair of boot moccasins from his saddlebag and slipped them on his feet, leaving his boots at the foot of one of the beds.

"What the hell are you doin' John?" Ben stood there, a pencil stuck behind his ear. Whit was sawing up strips of lumber that had already been measured.

"We'll bunk up in the mine for a time. Make us a fire down here, let it burn down. We'll take turns watching from the cave."

"You expectin' trouble?"

"Not right away, but just in case. We'll put rocks under these horse blankets so anyone sneaking up on us at night will think we're sleeping by the fire."

"Good idea," Ben said. "And them moccasins are your night slippers?"

"Tonight I'm going up creek, on the other side, to take a gander at the camp of those claim jumpers."

"What good will that do?"

"I'm going to count heads, see if I can hear what they might be planning."

"Want me to go with you?"

"No. You and Whit stay put, keep your eyes peeled until I get back."

"If I hear shootin' —"

"You'll hear shooting, that's all. Don't leave the cave, Ben."

"All right, if you say so."

"I say so."

"Johnny, I watched you grow from a gangly whippersnapper into a man with the bark on. But I'm still older'n you and a whole hell of a lot wiser."

"And I value your wisdom, Ben. I truly do."

"Well, you don't act like it. Goin' off on your own like this when we was always full partners."

"It's a one-man job, Ben. And you know me. I got a good memory for names and faces."

"Yeah, you do. When them bandits raided us, you 'membered every dang one of 'em. Faces and names."

"That's why I'm going alone up there tonight. I want to know what we're up against in case those prospectors have other ideas once their wounds heal."

"Aw, I think you drove 'em off for good."

"Ben, nothing's for good in this world. You cut off a snake's head, it can still bite you."

Ben snorted and walked back to where Whit was fitting pieces together and driving nails into wood.

"No, no, kid, you're doin' it all wrong. You get to work on a sluice box, and I'll build that first rocker. Hell, I drew you a dang picture."

"And the wind blew away what you drew, Mr. Ben."

"Don't call me Mr. Ben. It's just Ben, or Mr. Russell. And you don't call me that unless you got somethin' pretty important to say."

Whit nodded. "I know I can build that sluice box," he said.

"Just build one about two feet long for now. We got to start gettin' gold outen this crick by afternoon tomorrow."

"I'll do it, Ben."

Ben started hammering tenpenny nails into one of the rocker's side panels. Whit sawed a four-foot two-by-four in half, then another, while Ben glanced sidelong at him to see if the boy knew what he was doing.

John made coffee over a fire in the ring of stones up against the bluff. Ben opened tins of bully beef and peaches.

"Save those empty airtights," John said.

"What for?" Ben asked.

"I have a use for them."

The sun had crawled over the lower hills and mountains, was just sliding down behind the snowcaps when they finished eating.

"You coulda made some bannock or biscuits, John."

"Maybe tomorrow. I want to get you and Whit settled up in the mine and be on my way right after dusk."

"We sleepin' up there?" Whit said.

"You slept there," Ben said. "What's the matter? You didn't like it there?"

"It's cold and damp in that cave."

"Be glad you got a place to sleep, boy. Or maybe you want to go back home and sleep on a slat bed."

"Naw. I guess it'll be all right. I'd rather sleep by the fire, though."

"You sleep by this fire, you might never wake up, boy."

"Let it go, Ben. You've ridden Whit enough for one day. Your bedrolls are up there. Now, get on with it."

"Sure thing, Boss," Ben said, and the sarcasm in his voice brought a wry smile to John's lips. He picked up his rifle, checked his pistol, and walked to the creek. He waded across as Ben and Whit climbed the ladder to the mine. He looked back once, then disappeared into the aspen and the pines. The sun slipped down behind the western peaks and the clouds blazed with salmon and peach before they turned to ash. The blue faded from the sky and Venus winked in the darkened fabric of evening, a flickering silver star floating on a pale sea.

John stepped with care through the trees, stopping every so often to listen. His vision adjusted to the fading light as he crossed game trails and avoided noisy brush and downed limbs, his moccasins softening each footfall so that his journey was almost soundless.

He heard voices, and widened his course away from the creek until he was opposite the prospectors' camp, where firelight danced in orange tongues and men sat on logs, the smoke from their cigarettes and pipes swirling like fog in front of their orange faces.

He crept closer to the creek, hunched over, a step at a time, pausing, listening, trying to discern the words. When he got within twenty yards of the creek, he lay flat and crawled to a place where he could see the men's faces, hear their words without distortion.

"Not much color in my pan today," Krieger said. "Mighty disappointin', you ask me."

"Nobody asked you, Al," Pete said, a clay pipe stuck in his teeth.

"It's hard to pan with only one good arm," Krieger said. "When it's healed up, I aim to tack some hide to the barn door and set the door on fire."

"Don't brag about what you're gonna do, Al," a man said. "And I'll call that shot and all the others you might be thinkin' about."

John couldn't see the man's face. His back was facing him, but he determined that he was probably the leader. He saw Krieger, Rosset, and Short. The man they called Corny didn't say much, and there was one other, whose face and form were in shadow. He counted heads. Six men, and all but the one called Corny were packing six-guns, and there were five rifles close at hand, two leaning upright against the bluff, the others stacked on logs next to the men who owned them.

John retreated, crawling backward an inch

or two at a time. The sound of the creek drowned out any whispers from his clothing. He winced a time or two as pine needles poked his belly and legs, one of his arms. When he was far enough away, he stood up and walked back to camp, following the dark creek with its rippling waters off to his left. When he saw the glimmer of their campfire, he stopped and assessed its appearance. It looked as if two men were sleeping within yards of the fire, one on each side. Two dark lumpy shapes that might pass for him and Ben.

He had no doubt, after listening to the talk at the other camp, that the men he had shot carried grudges. And if the leader turned them loose, they'd be back. Apparently, they had brought extra rifles with them, which was not unusual. A man needed extra weapons in wild country. Five against two, if he subtracted Whit and Corny from the equation. Whit might be an extra gun if he could shoot. And Corny just might be a surprise if he took to bearing arms. Six against three, then, John thought.

Well, he had faced worse odds.

The moon rose and blazed a silver ribbon across the creek. John waded across the shallows and tossed another log on the fire before climbing up to the mine.

Somewhere above him, on the plateau, he heard the call of a timber wolf, and the sky was filled with stars as he reached the ledge, careful to make no sound.

"I see you, Johnny," Ben called from inside the cave.

"How do you know it's me?"

"I can smell you and them wet mockersons."

John chuckled and entered the cave.

9

They sat on tree stumps Manolo had set firmly in the ground to keep them from wobbling. He had placed five stumps around the front of the cabin. He sat on one, holding his tin cup with both hands, the coffee still steaming. Emma and Eva sat together a few feet away, drinking their coffee from tin cups. They wore old work dresses and lace-up boots, and their hair was bunched up in tight buns beneath faded kerchiefs.

"I guess Whit won't be back to help us with the garden, Manolo."

"No. It has been a week. Do you worry?"

"A little. I hope he's all right."

"He's in good hands, Ma," Eva said. "I'm sure John and Ben will take good care of him."

"I don't know," Emma said.

"Don't you trust them?" Eva asked, blowing on her coffee.

"After Argus, I don't think I trust any

man," Emma said.

"Not all men are like Argus," Manolo said.

"I was married to that man for twenty years, Manolo. And it turns out I didn't know him at all."

"Oh, Ma. John's a nice man. Just look at his eyes. You can tell."

"Don't you be lookin' at that man's eyes, young lady. You're too young to be flirtin' with any man."

"I'm nigh twenty years old, Ma. I can look at a man's eyes if I want to."

"Not that man's eyes."

"I notice you did your share of lookin' when he was up here."

Emma's face took on a rosy hue and she fanned herself with her hand.

"My, that coffee's hot," she said, changing the subject.

"He is handsome, Ma."

"Handsome is as handsome does. He killed your father. My husband."

"For good reason," Eva said.

Emma looked away from her daughter, out across the vast expanse of young grass, at the trees shining green in the early morning sunlight. The scent of evaporating dew and wildflowers filled her nostrils, and she saw faint mist rising from the grassy plain.

"A man who lives by the gun shall die by

the gun," Emma said, a dreamy expression on her face.

"I think you mean 'sword,' Ma."

"No, I mean gun. That man, John Savage, is a gunman. We saw enough of that kind in Denver."

"They weren't like John."

"He carries a gun, doesn't he? A gun that took Argus's life away."

"And it was a good thing he wore a pistol, Ma. Otherwise, Pa would have killed him. And maybe that poor girl, too."

"I don't want to hear any more about it, Eva. Now, Manolo, can you hook up that plow to one of the horses and plow us a garden?"

"You just tell me where, Miss Emma."

"A place that's close to the house and where the plants can get the sun all day. It would help if the ground was sloping a little."

"There is such a place," Pacheco said, "right over there, this side of the pine trees. The land rises there and your garden will drain."

"Good. Eva and I will get hoes out of the wagon and work the ground you plow, break up the clods before the sun dries them."

She looked over at the place where Manolo had pointed and saw that the ground did rise there, slightly, and it looked like a perfect place to grow vegetables.

"We'll finish our breakfast coffee and get to work," Emma said.

"And we won't either of us think about that handsome man John Savage all day, will we, Ma?"

"You watch your sassy little mouth, Eva."

Eva crinkled her nose at her mother and took another sip of coffee.

She knew they would both be thinking about John Savage until they saw him again.

And neither could wait until that day.

10

Whit hated the job Ben had given him. He worked bare-chested in the hot sun every day, shoveling gravel into the dry rocker he and Ben had built.

"We was goin' to work all this gravel when we was here before," Ben explained to Whit. "But we never got around to it. They's got to be dust a-plenty twixt the bluffs and the crick. You can make yourself some money, boy."

"When are you goin' to quit callin' me boy?" Whit snapped back at Ben.

"When you get some hair on your scrawny chest," Ben said.

He and John worked the sluice box, digging into the creek and shoveling water and gravel into the box, which was slanted on a large rock so that it had a steep slope. Color showed on the slats, and some wound up in the large pan set at the foot of the sluice box. Every evening, Ben washed the gravel, swirling it around in his large blackened pan until the gold clinging to the black dolomite shone like goldenrod.

The two men worked the stream, but they also paused often to listen. John had strung empty tin cans filled with small pebbles across every path leading to their claim. Anyone passing their way at night would not see the black string nor the cans stripped of their labels and painted black. Anyone tripping on the string would make a hell of a racket. But during the day, they were vulnerable and wary.

"I look for Carlos and Juanito any day now," Ben said that afternoon, when he was swirling sand around in his oversized pan, sloshing dirty water out over the lower edge every so often.

John, pouring clean stream water into the top of the sluice box, loosening the fine gravel so that it ran down the ladder, looked up and wiped his neck with a red bandanna, scowled at the sun falling from its zenith.

"Could be," he said, squinting to block out the sun from his eyes. "They're both good drovers and they have good help."

"You keepin' them on after they deliver the herd?"

"That was the plan. We'll have to plant hay right quick and winter wheat before the snow flies. And with those other folks living up there on our property, I reckon they'll have plenty to do. A lot of mouths to feed."

"Them Mexes won't take to pannin'."

"Two separate things, Ben. We dig for the gold, they tend to the herd and the crop."

"Yeah, but I seen what happens to men who see gold."

John laughed. He remembered. His first sight of gold in Ben's pan had sent a thrilling current through him as if he had touched a bolt of lightning. The beauty of it, so golden against the fine black grains of dolomite, was as intoxicating as any liquor, and the worth of it made it all the more appealing. And alluring.

"Yeah, I know. I'm not worried about Carlos or Juan so much as I am the other two he hired on. I can't remember their names."

"One's called Pepito, the othern's Gasparo, I think. Pepito is Juan's cousin. Gasparo herded sheep up in Wyoming."

"Yeah, but he likes cattle better, he told me."

"That man was hungry. He'd have said the same thing about herding cats or prairie dogs."

"You read a man pretty good, Ben."

"You got the same feelin'?"

John didn't answer, but dipped a pail into the creek and started running water through the sluice. He knew the spring runoff had brought down grains and nuggets of gold from somewhere higher up in the mountains, someplace near the mother lode, perhaps, where gold had been deposited many thousands of years before, or so he had heard. They already had an appreciable amount of dust and a few nuggets, weighty enough to put a few greenbacks in their pokes. And Whit had done his share, too, mining dust out of the dry sand. They hadn't had to do any crushing yet, and they hadn't laid a pick to the mine. That was hard work, and being up there brought back too many sad memories.

Gasparo Calderon, a burly, stocky man, with a face leathered and bronzed by the sun, rode into camp late in the afternoon. He wore two pistols on his hips, had another dangling from the saddle horn of the mouse-gray pony he called Chiva. He broke into a grin when he saw Ben and John, splashed across the creek in the shallowest part, and waved his battered felt hat as if he were attending a Saturday night foofaraw.

"Mr. Savage, we bring the cattle. They will be here tomorrow."

"Light down, Gasparo," John said.

"I got to get back. Carlos, he say to tell you he is coming."

"How many head?"

"Oh, more than a hundred, I think. Good cattle. Strong. Very fat, yes."

"How far away is Carlos camped?" John asked.

"I ride two hours. Maybe not far now. I find a place for him to bed down the cattle and left my bandanna to show him the place. I am very happy I find you. Do you have any whiskey? Any tequila?"

"No, we don't have any whiskey. You ride back and tell Carlos we'll meet him on the trail."

"First, John, I tell you something, eh?"

He rode up close to John and beckoned for him to come closer.

"What is it?" John said.

"There is a man watching you," Calderon whispered into John's ear. "He has the spying glasses." Gasparo cupped both hands and held them up to his eyes.

"Binoculars?"

"Yes, that is what he has. He did not know I see him hiding in the trees. When I see him, I ride a circle and come in so he do not know I am seeing him."

"Can you tell me where that man is now, without pointing?" John asked.

"He has built a ladder on a tall tree. He is in the top of that tree, maybe thirty *metros* from where you now stand. If you draw a straight line in the air, that is where he sits."

"Don't let him know you saw him when you ride back to Carlos."

"I will go the way I come. He will not know."

"Thanks, Gasparo. That is very useful information."

"What do you do? Do you kill this man because he is spying on you?"

"No, I won't kill him, but I sure as hell want to talk to him."

"Yes. I go now. *Adios.*" Calderon grinned at John and his eyebrows arched twice above his eyes.

Gasparo turned his cow pony and splashed across the creek, disappeared into the trees.

"What did that Mex tell you that I didn't hear?" Ben asked.

"If I tell you, Ben, don't let on, even to Whit. Got that?"

"Sure. What is it?"

"Gasparo spotted someone spying on us. I know just where he is. I'm going to walk upstream a couple of hundred yards and cross the creek at those shallows where the creek bends. You know the place."

"Yeah, way past where you got all them cans a-danglin'."

"That's the place. I want him to think I'm heeding a call to nature, so you go get me a couple of corncobs and holler something at me when I leave."

"Holler what?"

"I don't know. Make some joke about what I'm going to do in the trees."

"If you was goin' to take a crap, John, you'd go downstream, not up."

"I know that. Make a joke about that if you want. Yell real loud so he thinks I'm just going to drop my pants and squat."

"Then what?"

"Then, do what you were doing and make sure Whit stays at his task."

"I got it, Johnny. You're going to sneak up on that jasper and pull his rope."

"I'm going to find out what he's doing out there, sitting in a tree with a pair of binoculars, watching our every move."

"And if I hear shots from yonder, then what?"

"Then you'll know I couldn't talk the man down out of that tree. Now, go get those corncobs."

Ben went to the supply tent and walked back with two dried corncobs. He made a big show of handing them to John. John started walking upstream, away from camp. Whit looked up, but said nothing. He was still working the dry rocker, shoveling sand in it and shaking it until it rattled with gravel.

As John reached the aspens on their side of the creek, he heard Ben call out to him.

"Watch out a snake don't bite you on the ass, John."

John smiled and dropped the corncobs beside the path. Then he walked to the shallows and crossed without splashing or making any noise. It was quiet in the woods, and he made a wide circle, holding to his course by dead reckoning. When he was directly opposite their camp, a good two hundred yards from where he figured the spy to be, he began his silent stalk, heading straight for the tree where he figured the man was watching from.

It took him more than a half hour to reach the tree. He could see the man's back a good thirty feet up. He was sitting in a kind of cradle where the large limbs were thickest. John held his breath and watched the man put the binoculars to his eyes, then let them drop while he wiped his eyes and face with a blue bandanna. The man wore a pistol on his left hip. He was thin and wore dirty clothes. Beneath the tree, near a pair of spruce trees, John saw a crude lean-to, sawed branches on two forked limbs, with spruce boughs for a roof. No telling how long the man had camped there, but he was there for a reason.

The tree had thick limbs roped to it, making a crude ladder that the man could ascend and descend. He had not used hammer and nails, but carried the limbs from someplace out of earshot and painstakingly cross-tied each limb with heavy rope. Crude, but effective, John thought.

He started for the tree, a careful step at a time. He made every footfall soft and solid before he took another step.

When he was within ten yards of the tall pine tree, he stopped.

The man put the binoculars to his eyes, peered through the trees at their camp across the creek.

John grunted, imitating a bear.

He growled, low in his throat.

The man let the binoculars fall from his hands. It dangled there on his chest as he turned and looked down straight at John.

John drew his pistol.

The man appeared to swallow something in his throat. His Adam's apple stretched the skin on his neck and his eyes went wide as an owl's.

"Come down out of that tree," John said, "a step at a time, unless you want to take the shortcut."

"Sh-shortcut?" the man said.

"Yeah, straight down with your lamp out."

There was a long silence between the two men.

John cocked his pistol.

The sound was loud and unmistakable. It sounded like a key in an iron lock. Like a key turning on a door into eternity.

11

John stepped behind a pine tree, so that only part of his face and one arm with the pistol leveled at the man above him were visible.

"Snake out your pistol real careful, mister, and let it fall to the ground. Use two fingers. Anything else you do, I tick off this hair-trigger and blow your brains to mush."

"Yessir, d-don't sh-shoot."

The man gingerly picked his pistol from his holster, using two fingers on the butt. Then he let the six-gun fall. It hit the ground with a thud.

"Now, climb down out of there," John said. "Real slow."

John stepped out from behind the tree, walked over to the tall pine, picked up the man's pistol, and tucked it into his belt. Then he stepped back and watched the trembling man descend from his high perch.

When his feet touched the ground, the

man held on to the last wobbly rung of his makeshift ladder. His hands quivered and his knees touched as his legs trembled.

"Turn around," John ordered.

The man released his grip on the broken limb and its rope harness, turned slowly to face Savage.

John stepped closer, his pistol leveled at the man's gut. He saw the stain at the man's crotch, and the acrid reek of urine assailed his nostrils.

"D-don't shoot me, mister," the man pleaded.

John's nose crinkled up and he took a step backward to avoid the stench. A small puddle formed at the man's feet, and his face was blanched to a pasty prison pallor as the blood drained from every facial capillary.

"What's your name?" John asked.

"D-David Cornwall." He paused, licked his dry lips. "Th-they call me Corny."

"Who calls you that?"

"Al Krieger, Lem Thatcher, Walt Ferguson, and them. Men I work with."

"You with that bunch up creek, Krieger and two dimwits?"

"Yessir, we's prospectin' up yonder."

John regarded the man for several moments without speaking. The man was

107

plainly scared. John wondered why Krieger and his bunch had sent a coward to spy on him and Ben and Whit. The man probably had less brains than the three he'd already met. But a dunce with a gun was just as dangerous as a quick-witted man.

"You've been watching our camp for a few days, Corny. Now you're going to see it up close. Start walking toward the creek, and if you run, I'll drop you before your left foot hits the ground."

"What're you gonna do?" Cornwall asked.

"I don't know yet, Corny. We might eat you for supper. Now get moving. I hope you're through pissing because I don't want you stinking up our camp."

Corny started walking toward the creek, his binoculars dangling from his neck, bouncing off his lower chest with every step. He waded across the creek as Whit and Ben stood on the other side watching him as if he were something that had escaped from a zoo.

Sunlight glinted off the diamond-studded creek, and as the two men splashed across, tiny rainbows shimmered in the mist and droplets. Ben and Whit both saw the stain at Corny's crotch and knew it was not from creek water.

"You got yourself a pants pisser, John,"

Ben said as the men sloshed ashore. "I hope like hell you didn't scare anything else out of him."

John pulled Corny's pistol out of his waistband, handed it to Ben, butt first.

"See if it's loaded, then sit this spying sonofabitch down and keep him covered."

Ben took the pistol, put the hammer on half cock, and spun the cylinder.

"He's got five in the barn, John."

"I wonder if he's ever pulled the trigger," John said.

Ben herded Corny over to a log used as a bench, and made him sit down. He held the pistol a few inches from his face.

"You even look like a jackrabbit, son, and I'll put one of these .45s in your breadbasket."

"Whit, get his binoculars," John said, holstering his pistol.

"He smells like piss," Whit said.

"Know him?"

"He's one of the men up at that other mining camp. But he never beat me like Krieger did."

John walked over to Corny, looked down at the pathetic figure sitting there, still shivering. He felt sorry for the man, but what he had done was nigh unforgivable. The man had been spying on them, and he was a member of that bunch of claim jumpers. He might be stupid, but he was also dangerous.

"Who put you up to spying on us?" John asked.

"Lem Thatcher's the boss, I reckon. He told Krieger to tell me to come and spy on you boys, then, when they come for me, to tell 'em was you gettin' gold outen the crick and how much I figured you got."

"How long were you sitting up in that tree?"

"Four days, I reckon."

"Well, four days, or five, or six?"

"Took me a day near'bouts to rig that ladder and I couldn't make no noise. Al told me to be quiet and not get caught."

"So, how much gold do you figure we pulled out of the creek and ground in those four days?"

"I-I couldn't hardly tell. I mean, I couldn't see nothin' at night and not much during the day."

"So, what were you going to tell Thatcher and Krieger?"

Corny squirmed on the log, blinked his eyes three or four times, and tried not to look Savage in the eye.

"Look at me, Corny," John said. "What were you going to tell your thieving friends?"

"I-I reckon I was a-goin' to tell 'em I didn't know."

"That isn't what you were going to say."

"Pretty much."

"No, you were going to say we panned gold dust out of the creek and got gold from the rocker, weren't you?"

"I reckon you got some. More'n we been gettin'." He drew in a breath and stopped shivering. "Seems to me that's how it was."

"And what do you think Thatcher would do about it?"

Corny shook his head. "I don't know," he said.

"No, you know. They were going to jump us again, weren't they?"

Ben and Whit stood by, rapt over John's questioning. Ben held the pistol steady, but he seemed to have lost all desire to shoot the sniveling man in front of him who seemed about to cry or scream. Whit had a vacant look on his face, as if he were looking at some small animal caught in a steel trap.

Corny seemed to be wrestling with himself. He did not answer right away, but looked back up the creek as if expecting his companions to appear at any moment and start shooting. His hands trembled as he brought them to his face and covered it, as if he was shamed by being captured.

"You'd better start talking, Corny," John said, "or I'll tell Ben to put you out of your misery. I want to know what Thatcher and Krieger plan to do with the information you were going to give them."

Corny let his hands drop away from his face. The crown of his hat glowed tawny from the sun. A chipmunk skittered among the rocks and pebbles on the other side of the creek, its bristled tail quivering as if electrified, its tiny hands turning over stones as it looked for worms or grubs. A Steller's jay flickered, a streak of blue light, through the pines on the other side, squawking at another chipmunk squatting atop a rock at the edge of the trees.

"They ain't gettin' much gold from our claims," Corny said. "Thatcher said . . . he . . . said the spring runoff done carried most of it downstream, down here, I reckon. Crick's all burrowed out up thataway, and the rapids where the creek drops off has done carried all the gold down here."

"That's damned right," Ben said. "That's why we staked our claims at this spot. Creek widens here and them rapids is like one big sluice box, washin' the gold right down here into our pans."

John shot Ben a dark look.

"Lem Thatcher's pretty smart about such things. But last fall, when we all staked our claims, we saw a lot of color. We went down to the flat for the winter, down to Cherry Creek and Larimer Street. When we come back, it looked like all the gold had done washed down and got took away by them rapids."

"Gold can make a man crazy," John said. "A little color doesn't mean you're close to the mother lode."

Corny nodded, as if he was either in agreement with John or understood the wisdom of his observation.

"So, Thatcher aims to jump our claim," John said.

"I don't know. Honest."

"Honest, my ass," Ben said.

John shot him another reproachful look.

"Thatcher didn't send you to spy on us because he was just curious," John said. "He wanted to know if we were seeing color and filling our pokes."

"Yeah, I reckon," Corny said.

"Well, what were you going to tell him, Corny?" John drew his pistol, cocked it. He put it within inches of Corny's nose. "Be careful how you answer, because if I think you're lying, I just have to barely touch this trigger and you're wolf meat."

113

A beaded line of sweat broke out on Corny's forehead. He licked dry lips. His knees began to knock together. He tried to swallow, but his throat was as dry as his lips.

"I was goin' to tell Lem you was getting' gold out of the crick and from the sand," Corny said. "You got a good rich strike here, I figure."

John eased the hammer back to half cock and slid his pistol back into his holster. He turned his back on Corny and walked back and forth along the creek. Whit watched him and Ben kept his eyes on Corny. He knew John was thinking. Maybe pondering what to do with their prisoner.

John kicked a stone into the creek. It landed with a splash and the chipmunk scurried back into the trees. The jay flapped away like a blue rag blown by the wind.

He walked back over to Corny, stood next to Ben.

"Whit, you get back to work," John said.

"What're you gonna do with him, Mr. Savage?" Whit said.

"Just stay on that rocker, son."

"Yes, sir."

Ben looked at John.

"You got a big decision to make, Johnny. One I'm glad I don't have to."

"It's not a big decision at all, Ben. Krieger

and Thatcher opened the ball by sending this poor sonofabitch to spy on us. Blood's going to be spilled. It's damned sure not going to be mine."

"You aimin' to spill this Corny feller's blood?" Ben asked.

The rattle of the rocker filled the silence before John answered. Whit worked the box with unusual vigor. They could all hear the rustle of dry sand and the whisper of dust.

Corny made a small squealing sound in his throat. He looked at John with wide eyes brimming with the fresh tears of desperation.

John smiled at Corny. It was a dry mirthless smile that sent a chill up Corny's spine.

"Someone coming for you tonight, Corny?" John asked.

Corny nodded, unable to speak.

"Do you know who it will be?"

Corny shook his head.

"Then, we'll both find out, won't we?"

"You goin' to k-kill me, mister?" Corny's voice was a rasp out of his throat, brittle as the rustle of dry corn husks.

"I never shot an unarmed man in my life," John said. "But somebody's going to die tonight. Your friends opened the ball and now somebody's going to have the first dance."

115

A light breeze wafted down from the bluffs and stirred the ripples on the sun-shot stream. Golden colors seemed to mingle with the silver of the waters and, from the other side of the creek, the pine boughs swayed and the needles rubbed together like a drummer's brushes on a snare.

The sun was falling away in the sky and the night would be upon them soon. John looked up at the bluffs, the dark cavern of the mine, and the blue sky beyond, with white clouds drifting toward them like islands of cotton.

"Fetch some rope, Ben," John said. "Tie Corny's hands behind his back. Real tight."

Ben nodded and headed for the supply tent.

Corny pissed his pants again.

12

John led Corny to his small lean-to. The sun was setting, but there was still enough light for him to see clearly and assess his surroundings. The lean-to was a dozen yards or so from the laddered pine, and all around there was plenty of cover, with juniper, spruce, and fir trees scattered among the pines and the few stands of aspen near the creek.

"You sit or lie down there, Corny," John said. "And once I walk away, you keep your mouth shut. Don't talk to me. Don't ask questions. Just wait for whoever's coming to get you. Got that?"

"Yes, sir. I won't say nothin'."

"If someone calls out your name, you answer, that's all. If you try to warn the man, I'll shoot you dead."

"I won't say nothin'."

"Just call out the man's name if you recognize it and guide him to where you are. Simple enough?"

"Yes, sir. I'll just holler to let him know where I am."

"And say his name out loud."

"I can do that."

"You'd better."

"It'll be plumb dark when somebody comes to get me."

John gave Corny a withering look and started walking away to find a hiding place.

"I can see in the dark," John said.

He found a pair of junipers within ten yards of the lean-to. They were close enough together that he could fit between them when he sat down. One of the junipers looked as if it had been blasted with a cannonball. He recognized the ripped bark and broken limbs as coming from an elk rubbing the velvet from its antlers or practicing goring a rival bull. He sat down and scooted between the two trees, satisfied that his silhouette would not be visible in the darkness to come.

There was a blaze of color in the sky that lingered for some time, and then the clouds turned to ash and blackened before disappearing in the velvet sky, which soon blossomed with billions of stars. Corny made no sound, except when he changed position to relieve the strain on his buttocks. John could see his shape beneath the lean-to, a much darker blob than the surrounding shadows.

For a time, John could hear sounds from his camp, and he tried to picture what Ben and Whit were doing. He heard the crack of wood breaking as Whit chopped up kindling, the clank of a gold pan, the whickers of the horses a few hundred yards from where he sat, the tink of an empty can, the ping of a skillet on stone, and scraps of conversation, the words unintelligible.

He heard sounds he could not identify, and then it was quiet. He could hear Corny breathing, snuffling, squirming around as he tried to make himself more comfortable. He listened for the sounds that might reveal Corny working on his bonds, but there was nothing like the scraping or rubbing of rope against flesh.

The silence became immense as the mountains filled with deep shadows.

John felt every pine needle, every grain of dirt, press into his buttocks. Then, after a time, the flesh went numb. He heard a mule deer creep through the woods some distance away, the footfalls too light and cautious for an elk. A twig snapped and his senses jumped in alarm. Deer, he thought, or just the change in temperature as it fell. He fought off drowsiness and turned his head every few minutes to scan his surroundings for any alien sound. His nerves began to vibrate like a struck tuning fork as he strained to hear approaching footsteps. Whoever came for Corny would be almost blind from the darkness. He would make his way slowly and stop often to listen. John wondered if Corny had blazed the trail he took to get to the pine where he had sat looking across the creek at Savage's camp. He thought of the questions he should have asked, the trail he should have checked. He mentally kicked himself for not probing deeper into Corny's actions when he came to this spot.

He heard sounds from his own camp, rocks clanging together, the whispers of Whit and Ben. He craned his neck to see through the trees, and saw a glimmer of flame. He heard the plunk of logs and the fire grew higher and brighter. He knew what they were doing. They were making up the fake beds, using rocks under blankets to resemble two sleeping people. They were building up the fire so that it would last the night and illuminate the deceptive bedrolls.

How ironic, he thought. Corny would not have been able to see what Ben and Whit were doing in the dark, and unless he was smarter than he looked, he would not know of this nightly ritual. John could see the phantom wall of the bluff behind the dancing fire, and he thought he saw shadows, the shadows of men moving in front of the blaze. But he knew it was only an illusion, a ballet of shadows too far away to make out, a magic display of licking flames piercing the darkness, mere glimmers of something so far away and so shielded by the trees that only his imagination could see what might be happening.

John relaxed and turned his head away from the small flickers of firelight and looked over at the lean-to, hoping to glimpse Corny. It took him several moments to adjust his eyes to the darkness of the woods and the lean-to, and he thought he saw the silhouette of Corny, still sitting there, silent as stone.

He thought he heard Ben and Whit climbing the ladder to the mine, the faint creak of wood, the rustle of cloth, the incomprehensible grunts of two men reaching the precipice and padding toward the adit on worn boots and heavy soles. Did he hear those sounds? John did not know. But they, or what he thought he heard, faded from earshot and it was quiet again, except for the soft sigh of pine limbs brushing together in a light breeze and the crackle of dead wood contracting from the deep chill that whispered down from the high mountains, the snowy peaks bathed in darkness and chill far to the west.

John sighed and batted his eyes as he fought off drowsiness, the urge to lie down and close his eyes, sleep for just a while.

An hour of silence crept by, then another. He heard Corny rustling inside the lean-to, perhaps lying down and trying to fall asleep. He knew the man was still there. He could not have crawled away without making a lot of noise. And sounds carried far in the night in the thin mountain air. No, Corny was still there, but that black blob was now sprawled out flat beneath the spruce limbs of his shelter, and after a few minutes John heard the rattling sound of a man snoring.

Corny had fallen asleep and was not going to try to escape.

The snoring grew more regular, but not louder. Corny's snores had a lulling effect on John and he blinked in rapid succession, stretched his face and worked his mouth to stay awake, to listen beyond the snores, to drag in any sound from far away that seemed like a man making his way through the darkness and the trees.

He heard nothing but the drone of invisible insects, the scurries of small animals, the flap of an owl's wings as it floated like a dark scarf overhead.

The silence became acute and to John, it felt like the calm before a storm.

Someone would surely come for Corny. One man, or, perhaps, two, would walk through the trees to this spot and call out to Corny softly. One man only, perhaps, would call Corny's name. And Corny might awaken and call back and the man would hurry then, anxious to get his task over with and return to the comfort of his bedroll a mile or two up the creek.

That was the way John pictured it as he found new strength to avoid falling asleep. His senses were sharpened to a keen edge and when he looked toward his camp, he thought he saw the feeble tongues of fire-light splashing against the bluff, orange sparks rising in the night like fireflies.

Then he heard a sound that jarred his senses as if a gunshot had gone off next to his ear.

He stiffened and drew his pistol, snicked it out of his leather holster so fast he surprised himself.

Tin cans. The rattle of rocks in tin cans. The racket lasted only a few seconds, but to John it sounded like an army crashing through his ropes and makeshift signaling devices, ripping them loose from their moorings and dragging them along until they stopped clanking and were silent.

Gunshots broke the ensuing silence and he saw flashes of orange flame on the other side of the creek.

"Corny," he whispered. "Get over here. Crawl, run. Come to the sound of my voice."

The shots continued, volley after volley, and John heard hoofbeats. He saw shadows of men on horseback riding back and forth in front of the fire, their rifles aimed at the ground, fire spitting into the fake bedrolls, the whine of bullets caroming off rocks, the exultant yells and grunts of men bent on killing, blood in their eyes, hearts pumping like blacksmiths' bellows. And then, the firing stopped and he heard the throbbing sound of hoofbeats, the splashings of horses crossing the creek at a gallop.

Corny appeared on his hands and knees right in front of John. He grabbed Corny by the back of his collar and dragged him up between his legs.

"Lie down flat," he whispered, and pushed on the flat of Corny's back, driving him into the ground. "And don't make a sound."

He held Corny down with his left hand as

124

the woods exploded with the sound of charging horses. He could see their shadows as they made a beeline for Corny's camp.

"Corny," one of the men called.

Corny raised his head, and John shoved it back down.

"Yeah," John said, holding a hand over his mouth. "Over here."

He tried to imitate the sound of Corny's voice, but knew it would not make much difference. Voices were distorted at such a distance. The charging men would hear what they wanted to hear. They would hear Corny answering them.

"Come on, boys," Krieger said. "Corny's right up ahead."

Corny struggled to rise. John could feel the terror in the man's flesh as he pressed down on his back.

"Shhh," John whispered, and the silhouettes of horses and men drew ever closer, and the horses' hooves made a thunder that reverberated through John's bones. They came on and they fanned out, and he counted four men, four riders, and they were carrying rifles, rifles that looked like sticks in the dark, rifles that were black as bullwhips and stiff as iron rods.

The riders closed in on the lean-to and their rifles barked. Orange lances streamed into the fir boughs and bullets shredded limbs and gouged the ground inside the lean-to. The explosions were deafening as four rifles sprayed lead into the shelter, breaking the limbs that held up the roof until it came crashing down. The smell of exploded gunpowder filled the air, and white smoke billowed up into ghostly clouds as the riders encircled the collapsed shelter and kept firing until their rifles were empty.

"Come on, boys, foller me," a man said, and bounded off toward the mining camp up the creek. The other three men galloped after him.

John didn't recognize the man's voice, but he knew it did not belong to Krieger or the other two men he had previously encountered. This was the voice of a leader, and it was cold and hard and gruff, full of confidence and hatred.

It was the voice of a man who was not afraid to kill or be killed.

It was the voice of a man who would, from that moment on, be John Savage's enemy.

13

Ben thought, at first, that the mine was caving in on him. One minute, he was deep in sleep. The next, he heard the *clink* and *clank* of a dozen tin cans, the thunderous thump of hoofbeats, and the growling curses of men charging toward the camp below. He rose out of sleep with confused thoughts, gasping for breath.

Whit flung his blanket aside and sat up next to Ben.

"Wha . . . ?" he mumbled.

"Shut up, boy," Ben growled, low in his throat.

"My God, it sounds like —"

Ben clamped his hand over Whit's mouth and pushed him down on his bedroll. He grabbed his pistol up and crawled to the mine entrance, his senses full of clanging gongs as if a half dozen bell ringers were swinging on church ropes.

Horses dragged tin cans filled with stones

for a dozen yards, and then he heard the cans tumble away and come to rest. But the hoofbeats still pounded on sand and rock and earth, and he saw the dark silhouettes of men on horseback galloping toward the firelight and the two lumps resembling sleepers.

Whit crawled up next to him.

"You hush, boy," he whispered. "None of them claim jumpers know we're here."

He saw the golden gleam of Henry rifles as the riders swung them toward the fake sleepers. Then the riders opened fire, blasting orange flames, white smoke, and lead into the rocks beneath the blankets. The .44-caliber bullets ricocheted from rocks and whined off into the night. The fire caught strays and boiled with sparks that flew like exploding golden stars in all directions.

Ben couldn't see the faces of the men, nor see them fire into the blanket-covered rocks, because he was too far from the ledge, but he knew what they were doing and, with Henry rifles, they did not have to reload very often. Each of those rifles would hold sixteen rounds in their magazines.

Moments later, he saw the riders cross the creek, splashing water droplets gleaming like fireflies, and then they were in the woods, riding single file in a straight line. The very path John and Corny had taken hours before. His heart caught in his chest and he felt it squeezed from some unseen hand.

"Golly, Ben," Whit gasped, "those men were tryin' to kill us down there."

"They thought that, sure as hell."

"We got to get out of here."

"You just stay right where you are if you want to live. This old mine saved my life once before, and I'm damned sure not gonna give it up now."

"Where are they goin'?" Whit asked.

"Right where John and Corny are waitin' for them," Ben said.

"They goin' to kill John?"

"Just shut up, will you, kid?"

Ben waited, his breath stilled in his chest, seconds ticking away in his mind. Minutes crawling by like a column of ants scratching his skin.

That old nemesis, fear, began to creep through Ben's brain. He felt the first tightening of his stomach muscles, then the quivering signs of buck fever in his legs. He realized that those four men had ridden up on their camp with the intent to kill, to murder him and John in their sleep. No hesitation. No mercy. He gulped in air and clenched his fists. Fear did not belong here.

Not now. He was still alive. John's ruse had worked. Putting those rocks under blankets to resemble sleeping men, and those rattling cans as warning signals. All John's ideas. And they had worked.

But, he thought then, what about John and that skinny drink of water named Corny? Did those claim jumpers go after Corny to take him back to their camp? He hadn't seen a spare horse. What did they mean to do?

Then he spoke softly to Whit.

"They don't know John is out there in the woods," he said.

"They goin' after that Corny feller?"

"Maybe," Ben said.

And then, he stiffened as he heard the crack of Henry rifles. He listened intently, not counting the shots, but listening for the bark of John's .45 Colt. He heard a crashing sound, but no screams. Only more gunfire from those Henrys, and then a sudden silence. After that, the thump and thunder of hoofbeats. Horses galloping away through the trees, heading up creek. Then the sounds faded and ceased as if swallowed up by the night itself.

"Ben —"

"Shut up, kid. Let me think."

"I think John and that Corny are plumb
—"

"Don't you say it, kid. Unless I see John
stretched out with my own eyes, he ain't
dead, you hear?"

"Yes, sir."

After a while, as they lay there, both listening, Ben said, "Shit."

"They're both dead, ain't they?" Whit said.

Ben got to his feet.

"I'm going out there for a look-see," he
said, walking over to his gunbelt coiled up
like a snake next to his pillow. He picked it
up and slid his pistol back in his holster.

"You stay here, kid," he said, strapping on
his gunbelt. "If I ain't back in an hour, you
go get your horse and ride back home."

"I want to go with you, Ben. I can't do no
good here."

"You can't do no good nowhere, kid."

Ben started climbing down the ladder,
stopping at every rung to listen, to look both
ways up and down the creek. He saw Whit
peering down at him from the edge of the
precipice.

"This is why we sleep with our boots on,"
he said, descending to the next rung.

"You be careful, Ben, hear?"

"I hear you, boy."

"I wished you'd quit callin' me boy."

131

"I wish you'd learn to keep your trap shut."

And then he was down on the ground and he didn't look back up.

Instead, he looked at the shredded blankets, the gleaming brass shells of expended .44 cartridges, the blasted campfire, with faggots blown out of the fire ring smoking and glowing with every fan of breeze. Hoofprints in the sand and gouged-out dirt in scattered clumps. It looked as if a storm had come through and ravished just that one spot where the blankets were in bullet-riddled tatters.

That fear was still with him as he waded across the creek, a careful step at a time. He dreaded what he would find in the woods. He didn't want to think about it, but it was all he could think of as he stepped into the trees and into the leaden shadows of night.

He did not draw his pistol, but he kept his right hand on the butt of his Colt .45, ready to draw and shoot.

He heard something slither along the ground, through the pine needles and the brush. He heard the horses whicker softly, and they sounded as if they were in a far country. Every shadow looked ominous, every tree hid a man with a rifle, and each bush was a crouching animal or a bloodthirsty man. He was sweating and the air was chill.

It seemed he could still hear the hoofbeats of those horses galloping toward the claim jumpers' camp. Echoes? Only in his mind, a mind that was cloudy with fear and disjointed from doubt and apprehension.

He stopped, leaned against a pine tree.

There, he became disoriented. He looked back toward the glowing campfire, and it danced around like a summer mirage.

He listened to the sound of his own breathing, and it was shallow and fearful, the way it had been when he was a boy entering a haunted house at the urging of his companions. Silly, he thought. He looked up at the sky, at the stars shining through pine branches, winking silver and cold like millions of eyes that were unfeeling and uninterested. He felt very small and alone, as if he were the only man on earth left alive after some terrible disaster.

He stopped looking up and looked down at the ground. He could hardly see it, but he knew it was there. He moved his boot and heard the scraping noise it made. That seemed to pull him back to reality, to establish where he was.

Ben wanted a cigarette or a chaw of tobacco, a pipe between his teeth, a shot of raw whiskey. Anything that would take away the grabbing claws of fear, the oncoming dread that was like some giant shadow descending on him. Dread of finding John dead. John and Corny. Shot to pieces and lying like bloody rags in the pale wash of starlight, silent and unbreathing.

He started to step away from the tree and continue on, conquer his fear and his dread. He took one step, and then froze as his veins turned to ice and something crawled down his back.

A sound like a footstep.

Elusive, but . . .

And then, there it was again. Another sound, the careful step of something heavy. Man or beast? He did not know. But he clamped his hand on the butt of his pistol and began to ease it out of its holster.

"Wh-who's there?" he called as his pistol cleared leather.

And his voice came from somewhere else, from someone else, low and gravelly, full of fear and dread as if he was expecting the Grim Reaper to appear before him, carrying a long-handled scythe to chop his head off with one whirring sweep of a deadly blade.

14

John waited not only until the hoofbeats faded away, but also until the deep silence of the mountains returned to that small spot where he sat, his left hand still plastered to Corny's back, his right hand gripping his pistol, which was as cold and lifeless as the blanket of cold breeze that now enveloped him. He had not fired the pistol. Had he done so, he realized, he would have been outgunned. He would be lying dead now, perhaps atop a dead Corny, and none would know of their passing until morning.

He slipped his pistol back into its holster as he lifted his hand from Corny's back. The danger had passed, and he still had an unwanted prisoner. Corny drew in a breath, but did not try to rise. Instead, he lay there, shivering like a vagabond child in winter, a small whimper escaping from his lips like the mewling of a wet kitten.

"Not a word, Corny," John whispered as

he stood up. He reached down and grasped the back of Corny's collar and pulled the man to his feet. "Not one damned word, you hear?"

Corny nodded and stood there, shaking, wobbly on his feet, like a colt newly born, his spindly legs nothing more than unreliable props under a fragile and untested body.

John cupped Corny's elbow and guided him over to the shattered lean-to. He stooped down and picked up two brass shell casings, showed them to his prisoner.

"Recognize these, Corny?"

"They got Henry Yellow Boys. Them are shells from those."

"Those men didn't know I was here. They thought you were catching some shut-eye under that lean-to you built."

Corny gulped and gasped. "I know," he whispered.

"Seems to me you've got some tall thinking to do, Corny."

"Y-yessir."

"Come on. Back to my camp for some palaver."

He pulled Corny away from the lean-to and headed him toward the creek, walking by his side. After a few minutes, he stopped. He put a hand over Corny's mouth.

"Don't make a sound," he whispered in Corny's ear. "I'll be right back."

John left him there and took a few steps ahead. He stopped, listened, then took more steps, careful to make no noise.

A few minutes later he saw a familiar shape leaning against a tree. Beyond, he saw the faint glimmer of their campfire, shadows crawling over the stark bluff, the glint of starlight on the creek.

He saw Ben draw his pistol, and smiled. He continued his quiet stalk until he was only a few feet away from his friend. He slid behind a pine tree and spoke.

"Put your pecker away, Ben," he said, and watched Ben jump and whirl.

"John? That you?"

"If that's not your pecker, you can put it back in its holster."

"Damn, you scare a man half to death. I thought you was —"

"Wait here," John said.

A few minutes later, he came up with Corny in tow.

"You ain't dead, neither," Ben said to Corny. He was sweating like a horse at a county race.

"Let's get back to the mine and sort this all out," John said.

Corny stumbled along between them, his

hands still tied behind his back. They crossed the shallows and stood by the shot-up campfire, looking at the shredded blankets, the bullet-scarred rocks, the gouges in the sand, the pockmarks on the bluff's face.

A white face appeared, peering over the precipice.

"That you, Ben?" Whit asked.

"Be up in a minute, kid. Keep your shirt on," Ben said.

The face disappeared.

John pulled his knife from its scabbard on his belt and cut Corny's bonds.

Ben's eyes widened, and his mouth opened in surprise.

Corny felt his hands drop free. It took him a moment to realize what had happened, and then he slowly brought his hands around to his front and started rubbing his wrists.

"You're free to go on back up to your camp, Corny," John said.

Ben spluttered.

"You lettin' that murderin' scalawag loose, John?"

"He has his choice," John said. "He can go back to his bunch or throw in with us."

"You've gone plumb loco, Johnny," Ben said.

John looked Corny in the eye, measuring the man, waiting to see if he had any backbone at all.

"I ain't goin' back with them," Corny said. "But I got nothin' to offer you, neither."

"John —" Ben started to say.

John held up his hand to stop Ben from protesting.

"I'll have cattle up on the plateau by tomorrow night," John said to Corny. "Be a lot of work, and little pay. You might pan some with us on slow days and earn yourself a little pocket money. I can probably give you a bedroll and grub. That's about the size of it."

"I-I'll stay with you, mister. I can't go back to them."

"What the hell?" Ben said, scratching the back of his bare head.

"That bunch tried to kill Corny here, Ben. They probably think they killed all of us."

"Why'd they try to kill their own man, you reckon?"

"I think we got us a pretty bad bunch up creek," John said. "Maybe they wanted to put the blame on Corny for killing us. Or maybe they had no more use for him. What do you think, Corny?"

Corny heaved his chest as he drank in air. He shook his head solemn-like and his eyes got wet.

"Thatcher," he said, "is as mean as they come. They say he once rode with Quantrill and murdered some folks back in Illinois. Him and Krieger and Ferguson stretched a man's neck up in Wyoming about a month ago when he caught them cheatin' at cards. So, I don't reckon they got much use for me."

"How'd you get hooked up with them?" John asked.

"I was swampin' at a saloon on Larimer Street over to Denver. Them boys come in all the time, made it their private waterin' hole. One day, they said they was goin' prospectin' and said they could use a hand to cook and wash their clothes and such. They put a double eagle in my hand when I was flat broke and I just took up with 'em. I found out later that they killed two men in Cherry Creek and stole their minin' claims. Thatcher said if I ever told anyone, he'd cut out my gizzard."

"So, he had a reason to kill you tonight," John said.

"I told him I would never tell nobody about what him and Ferguson done."

"You can't trust a man like that," Ben said.

"No, I reckon you can't," Corny said.

"Grab up some of those shot-up blankets,"

John said to Corny, "and climb that ladder up to the mine. Ben, you help him."

"You think they'll be back tonight?" Ben asked.

"No, but they'll be back. Unless we get them first."

"Huh?" Ben scowled.

"I know one thing, Ben. It's no longer a case of live and let live. Thatcher and his bunch have attacked us. He wants our claim. He didn't ask to buy it, or trade for it. He was just going to take it. If we'd been sleeping down here, we'd be dead now. And they'd be picking us clean in the morning, like a flock of buzzards."

"So, what do you aim to do?"

"I'm going to have to think on that, Ben."

"For how long?"

"Not long, I reckon. First off, I want to find a way to let Thatcher know that we're still alive. Give him something to chaw on for a time."

"And then what?"

"I guess that one day I'll have to call the bastard out."

"A man who sneaks up on a sleepin' man in the dark ain't gonna mix in a fair fight, Johnny."

"No, he's not. I said I was going to think about it. I want him to think about something, too."

Corny was gathering the riddled blankets, tucking them under one arm.

"What's that?" Ben asked.

"I guess I want him to think about hell."

"Hell's a long way off," Ben said.

"Not his hell. It's real close."

"Sometimes, John, you plumb give me the shivers. I thought we was through with all that when we rubbed out Hobart."

"As long as there are men like Thatcher, we won't ever be through with it. I can see that now."

"Once't you thought that gun of yours was cursed. Do you still think it is?"

"I don't know, Ben. Maybe it's me that's cursed. You go on up to the ledge with Corny. I'll be along directly."

Ben turned and guided Corny to the ladder. "Here, give me one of them blankets," he said, and grabbed one. "You climb on up, Corny. I'll be right behind you."

The two men started climbing the ladder. Whit waited for them.

John walked some distance from the fire and looked at the bubbling creek with its dark waters, its riffles shining with stars. He looked around, beyond to the trees and downstream where the waters disappeared.

The darkness changed everything, he

thought. It carved out its own shapes and made a man look up at the sky and feel small. It also brought out the hunters and the prey. He was tired of being prey for men like Thatcher and Ferguson. He didn't like killing, but he didn't like being hunted, either.

He knew that it would not be easy to fight those men up creek. They were dangerous. And they were men who had no conscience.

Those were the worst kind.

They weren't afraid to kill and they weren't afraid to die.

Such men had no feelings whatsoever.

They were just men without souls, without hearts.

He tapped the Colt on his hip.

Maybe it did carry a curse in its iron muscles, its veins.

If so, he thought, he hoped that curse would hold for the days ahead.

He looked up at the stars and walked back to the dwindling fire, looked at the scarred rocks where bullets had ricocheted or flattened to lumps of lead.

Then he began to climb up to the cave that had once saved his and Ben's lives.

15

Eva awoke to an empty house. The logs and floors ticked with that emptiness. Her mother's bed was made, and she smelled the heady aroma of Arbuckle's coffee, the faint scent of cinnamon. Her mouth was pasty with night phlegm and, as she dressed, her stomach groaned with the sounds of hunger.

"Ma," she called as she laced up her boots. The edge of her small cot creaked as she stood up, releasing her weight.

There was no answer, and Eva felt a wave of apprehension wash through her, tightening the muscles in her abdomen and cloaking her senses with a vague feeling of abandonment.

The cabin still reeked with the smell of pine and the logs, with their pine knots, made her feel as if they were eyes watching her. She wished they had pictures or samplers to hang on the walls, calendars, even, to cover those pine knot eyes. She walked outside and felt better for it. It seemed so quiet and peaceful with all that land stretching out and greening up, the trees so green they shone like emeralds in the sunlight.

Her mother was sitting on a felled tree near the fringe of the woods, a tin cup of steaming coffee in her hand. Her mother almost never made coffee for herself, only for Manolo or her father, when he had been at home. Yet there she was sitting on that log, her long dress covering her legs, a faded shawl over her shoulders. She looked old and tired, Eva thought, hunched over like that, staring down the long valley.

"Ma," Eva called.

Her mother turned and held up a hand. Then, she beckoned to her daughter with a slight movement of that same hand, and Eva walked toward her.

"What are you doing out here all by yourself, Ma?"

"I am by myself. Manolo's way down there and you were fast asleep."

"And drinking coffee. You almost never drink coffee, except when Pa's home."

"I felt like coffee this morning. I had a restless night."

"Dreams?"

"No, well, some, I guess, but I can't

remember them much. Noises. Imagined noises, maybe."

"What kind of noises?" Eva sat down beside her mother, brushing the bark of the tree in case there were spiders or eggs or grubs on it. They were in the sun so she was not cold, although she wore a thin muslin shirt and a cotton dress with daisies on it, no stockings.

"I thought I heard firecrackers, you know, like those we always heard on the fourth of July, when we lived in Shreveport."

"I hated Shreveport," Eva said.

"Well, that's what it sounded like. The sounds were very faint, and I walked outside in my nightgown and did not hear them again."

"So you went back to sleep?"

"No, I couldn't sleep. I made coffee and thought about cherry trees and persimmons and how we could never have them up here. Even the garden we planted is a sorry one. We can't plant pumpkins or watermelons up here."

"We planted corn and beans and peas and radishes, cabbage. Isn't that enough?"

"We don't know what winter is like up here, Eva, but we know the spring and the summer will be short. Manolo said this will all be covered in snow for months and noth-

146

ing we plant can grow past the first snow."

"Did Manolo hear the firecrackers?"

Emma turned her head to look at Eva.

"He did. He said they were gunshots. Far away. He said that sounds carry far up in these mountains at night."

"Gunshots?"

"That's what he said. There were a lot of them. I couldn't figure out where they were coming from, but Manolo could."

"Where were they coming from?"

Emma pointed to the edge of their world, where the valley table sloped and disappeared.

"He said down by the creek. Where Whit is. Where those two men are. There were a lot of shots, if that's what they were."

"Manolo was sure they were gunshots? Maybe they were firecrackers."

"Manolo said gunshots and he marked the time. Late. Before midnight. I'm worried about Whit. Maybe those men shot him. Killed him."

"Ma."

"I just don't know, Eva." She sipped her coffee and stared toward the end of the valley. Eva looked and saw something move. She squinted her eyes and shaded them from the sun.

"There's Manolo now," Emma said.

Eva saw Manolo walking out of the woods. He carried a scattergun, an old one her father had given him, what he had called a "Greener." It was double-barreled and the sun glinted off those patches where the bluing had worn off, exposing the silvery metal.

Emma stood up. Manolo was breaking into a run, waving one arm above his head.

"Look, Eva."

Eva stood up. "He's running," she said. "And waving."

"My heart's nigh stopped," Emma said.

"It looks like he's smiling, Ma."

Emma put a small fist to her chest, over her heart.

"I feel faint," she breathed.

Eva put her arm around her mother to keep her from toppling over.

"Don't faint, Ma."

"They are coming," Manolo shouted.

"Who's coming?" Emma said, recovering from her near swoon.

"I don't know," Eva said. "Maybe Whit and John and Ben."

"Whit?"

Emma sounded addled.

Manolo was still some distance away, but he was running fast. He was no longer waving his arm. He bounded over the grass like a deer, his shirttail flapping, the brim of his straw hat bending back against the crown.

"They are coming," he yelled again. "The cattle."

"The cattle?" Emma said.

Eva thought for a moment.

"Of course," she said. "John said he was bringing a herd of cattle up here. That must be what Manolo's yelling about."

"Oh, my," Emma said. "Cattle. Why, yes, of course. I just didn't expect them so soon."

"He said about two weeks. Whit has been gone about that long, Ma."

"Is Whit coming with them?"

"I don't know," Eva said, and then Manolo was in front of them, panting and grinning.

"Where are they, Manolo?" Emma asked.

"They are coming from that other valley, lots of cattle. I saw them. Many of them."

"Did you see Whit?" Emma asked.

"No, I do not see him. But there are men driving the cattle and they are coming this way."

"What about John and Ben?" Eva asked. "Did you see them?"

Manolo shook his head.

"No, just the cattle and some Mexicans driving them. They are in no hurry. But there are many of them."

"Well, get yourself a drink of water, Manolo, or have some coffee. There's a pot on the stove, still warm, I expect."

"No, I wait for the herd. But I will put the shotgun away."

"Manolo," Eva said, "did you hear firecrackers last night?"

"No. I did not hear the firecrackers. I hear the gunshots. Many of them. I think they come from the creek. I could not tell. Many shots and then I heard nothing."

"You're sure they were gunshots?" Eva asked.

"Yes. I am sure. I thought it was an army."

Eva sighed, waved Manolo away. He trotted off toward the cabin.

"Do you believe me now, Eva?"

"Yes, Ma, but John and Ben might have been shooting at targets."

"In the middle of the night?"

"Maybe bears."

"Whit said he was beaten up by some mean prospectors. Maybe —"

"Ma, you're just guessing. I'm sure when we see John again, he will clear it up."

"You can't get that man out of your mind, can you, Daughter?"

"What about you, Ma? You mention his name a dozen times a day."

"I do not," Emma snapped.

"You do, too. I think —" Eva clamped her mouth shut, afraid of what she might say.

"What do you think?"

"Nothing," Eva said.

"You're sweet on that man, aren't you?"

"I am not. But you are."

Emma's face flushed.

"You watch your mouth, young lady."

"What are you going to do? Slap me?"

"I just might."

"Then, you do care about John Savage, don't you, Ma?"

Emma's expression turned livid. Her lips flattened against her teeth and her eyes flashed fire. She raised her cup and, for a moment, Eva thought her mother was going to throw hot coffee on her. Instead, Emma just glared at her daughter in raging silence, the anger in her seething just below the surface of her countenance.

"That man killed your father, Eva. My husband. Don't you ever forget it."

Eva seethed, too, but controlled herself by breathing through her nose.

"It doesn't matter, Ma, who killed Pa. He was a bad man and he deserved to die."

Emma raised a hand as if to slap her daughter, but something caught her eye. She turned and looked down the plateau. A few head of cattle were streaming in from the trees, but beyond, at the far edge of the tableland, three figures on horseback emerged on the horizon.

"Is — is that Whit?" she stammered, her eyes squinted to dark slits.

Eva turned to look. She saw the cattle and then the three riders. More cattle ambled onto the grasslands and began to fan out. The figures on horseback grew larger.

"Yes, Ma, that's Whit. He's riding up with John and Ben."

"Are you sure?"

"Pretty sure. Who else could it be?"

"Oh, my goodness. I look a fright." Emma patted her bunned hair and turned toward the cabin. She broke into a trot. Then she turned her cup over and emptied it as she ran.

"See, Ma, you do care about John," Eva called after her.

Emma didn't answer. In a few moments, she disappeared inside the cabin. Manolo walked around the house and headed toward Eva. He no longer carried the shotgun, but had changed into a clean shirt. He slept in a small three-sided hut in back of the house. He was still building on it in his spare time.

Eva wondered if she should put on some perfume or rouge her face and lips. No, that would be too obvious, she thought. Let her mother throw herself at John Savage for all she cared. She remembered that first look between them. John looking at her, she looking at John. She burned now with the memory of it. That look, she thought, she would never forget it. That look was forever.

Her heart beat fast as she waited to see John again.

Her stomach was full of fluttering butterflies and her pulse raced like a thundering wind at her temples. She took in a full breath of air, and her chest swelled under her dress as Manolo came up beside her, silent as a cat.

"So, he is coming," Manolo said, softly and with a rare tenderness.

"Who?" Eva said, flustered at Manolo's perception.

"The tall man. The handsome one. The one you wait for."

"Mind your place, Manolo," Eva said. "You don't know anything."

"I know what is in your heart," he said. "And, I think, so does he."

"You just mind your own business, Manolo."

He laughed and took off his hat. He bowed and swept the hat in front of him.

"Yes, miss. I mind my own business. But my eyes see what my eyes see."

He started walking toward one of the

drovers who was herding the cattle across the plain.

Eva watched him and thought how wise Manolo was. And if he could see what was in her heart, so could her mother.

And so, too, would John Savage.

16

John's heart thrummed in his chest when he saw the cattle spreading out over the grassy plain. They were, as Gasparo had said, fat on winter hay, and the short drive up from the Denver stockyards had not leaned them down much. He saw Carlos Montoya and waved. Carlos waved back, yelled at a small bunch of white-faced Herefords, and then turned his steeldust gray and galloped toward him.

"*Hola*, John," he said as he rode up.

"You made good time, Carlos. Lose any?"

"No, we no lose any, and soon you will have two cows to milk. They are coming with their calves."

John stood up in the stirrups and hollered back over his shoulder.

"Okay, Gasparo, come on up, and bring Corny with you."

Gasparo had ridden to their camp early that morning and said that Carlos was crossing the creek at the wide shallows about two miles from camp. He guessed they would reach the plateau in about three more hours, but the herd was strung out for another three miles or so, and it would take most of the day to get them all up on the new pasture.

John, Ben, and Whit had set out, with Corny and Gasparo bringing up the rear. He told Gasparo and Corny to wait below the plateau until he called them up. He wanted to make sure that they had not been followed and that the claim jumpers were not waiting for them. Corny had said that they knew nothing about the cattle or their homestead, but John still didn't trust him.

The two men rode up, Gasparo grinning like a Mexican Cheshire, and Corny's eyes bulging out of their sockets like hen's eggs.

"The wagons should be here before the sun sets," Carlos said.

"Juanito is driving the chuck wagon," Gasparo said.

"And Pepito, he drives the supply wagon," Carlos said.

"Good job, Carlos," John said.

"And there is gold?" Carlos said, a smile on his thin lips. He was lean and wiry as a cougar, with a pencil-thin moustache and long sideburns. He, like the other drovers,

156

wore two six-guns on his belt and had another dangling from his saddle horn. A Henry Yellow Boy jutted from his saddle scabbard. John knew that all were fully loaded. He had picked his drovers well. They were all good *vaqueros* who had learned about cattle from Argentine *gauchos* when they were boys in Jalisco. They also knew the ways of the West and the scorn of the white men. They had come up from Texas and liked what they saw when they looked at the snowcapped mountains and the sprawling empty lands.

They saw opportunity and John, who spoke fluent Spanish, made friends with them, told them of his plans.

He told them he would build a ranch and give them a place where they could raise their families.

"It will be a democracy on my ranch," John said, "but I am the boss."

"Democracy," Carlos had said, "is a word found only in the dictionary. Discrimination is found everywhere we go."

"There is no discrimination in the mountains, Carlos," John had told him. "There are only men who know how to live on the land."

"We will see," Carlos had said.

"That is my promise to you. You will be

treated as a man when you work for me. You can be Mexican or Russian, I don't care."

The two men shook hands and Carlos helped him pick out the stock and hired the hands. None of the men were married, but they all were young and intended to find mates when they had built homes and had money in their pockets.

More cattle ambled into the valley. Carlos spoke to Gasparo. *"Vete a los ganados,"* he said, and Gasparo nodded, rode off toward the woods to help the drovers drive the rest of the herd into the valley.

"Good grass," Carlos said, looking around. "Very young and tender yet."

"Growing fast," Ben said.

John turned to Whit.

"Go on, Whit. Ride up to the cabin and see your ma and your sister. We'll pick you up later."

"Thank you, sir," Whit said. He turned his horse and rode off.

Ben shaded his eyes and looked toward the cabin.

"That young Eva's standing out there, a-lookin' at us," he said to John.

"I saw her," John said.

"We have brought some lumber, hammers, nails, saws," Carlos said. "You just tell me where to start the building."

"I will," John said, "but first, I want to fill you in on some trouble that may lie ahead."

"Trouble?" Carlos said. "I do not like trouble."

"I think I can handle it, but you have to know what Ben and I ran into down at our diggings."

"Tell me," Carlos said in Spanish.

John told him about his run-in with three claim jumpers and the events of the previous night. Carlos kept looking at Corny while John was talking.

"You keep this man?" he said when John was finished. "You should shoot him or hang him."

"I don't think he knew what he was getting into with that bunch, Carlos. I think he'll make a good hand."

"He will work with me and my men?"

"If you want him to," John said.

"I will think about it, John."

"Well, don't think too long, Carlos. There's a lot to do, and we'll need every hand."

"*Bueno.* With Corny and that young boy, we have two more than we thought."

"Three, maybe," John said. "Mrs. Blanchett has a man working for her, Manolo Pacheco. That's him over there chasing those cows to pasture."

Carlos looked and saw Manolo. "Ah, *un paisano,*" he said. "Three, then."

"And Emma Blanchett and her daughter live up there in that cabin. They can help with the chuck, maybe. They're all working for me."

"And then, you are already a rich man, John. You have found much gold, eh?"

"Enough to cover some expenses," John said guardedly.

"I think you are *muy rico,* John. I can see it in your eyes. And I can smell gold."

"You're not smelling any on me yet."

"Maybe those *bandidos* want to steal it, eh?"

"They might try," John said.

"Do you want us all to go with you to their camp and help you shoot them?"

John pulled in a long breath.

"That would be lawless," he said.

"Are you not the law in this place? I do not see any sheriffs. I do not see no constables. I do not see no judge."

"As a last resort, maybe I am the law. But so are they, in their minds."

"John, John, you talk like a woman. Do not wait for them to attack you again. You must cut off the head of the rattlesnake before it bites you, not after it has put the poison in your blood."

"He's right, John," Ben said. "We ought to ride up to Thatcher's camp and rub ever' damn one of those boys out."

"That's not as easy as it sounds, Ben. Every one of those men is armed and primed to shoot."

"We could sneak up on 'em at night like they done to us," Ben said.

"Yes, that would be a good way," Carlos said.

"Carlos, you tend to the cattle. I'll worry about Thatcher and his bunch."

"Uh-oh," Corny said, twisting his head, "speaking of the devil. Look over yonder way to the other side of the valley. Just in the trees. I think I know who that is."

Ben and John looked and saw a rider, just barely, sitting his horse, watching them.

"You got those field glasses we took off Corny in your saddlebags, Ben?" John asked.

"Sure do."

"Give them to Corny. Corny, you take a gander and see if you recognize that rider."

Ben pulled the binoculars from his saddle-bag and handed them to Corny. Corny held them to his eyes and adjusted the lenses.

"That's Pete Rosset," he said.

"Anybody with him?" John asked.

Corny scanned both sides of the horse and rider with the binoculars. He shook his head.

"Nope, just Pete. But he's packin' iron. Six-gun on his hip and a rifle in his boot."

John took the binoculars from Corny, set them on Pete Rosset.

"I recognize him," John said. "Well, the cat's out of the bag now. Thatcher will soon know we're up here, and he'll —"

"He'll what?" Ben said.

"I don't know what he'll do. But he'll do something. Meanwhile, let's let old Pete know what for."

John drew his Winchester from its scabbard, levered a cartridge into the chamber, and dropped the front blade sight on Rosset. He lined the blade up with the rear buckhorn and took a breath, held it.

"Don't shoot," Carlos said. "You might stampede the cattle."

John lowered the rifle. He had been just a finger tick away from pulling the trigger.

"You're right, Carlos. We might have a week's work ahead of us if I spooked those cattle."

"Aw, shit," Ben said. "You had him cold."

As the four men watched, the rider turned his horse and disappeared in the trees.

"Maybe he got the message, anyway," John said.

"He should have carried a lead pellet in his belly back to Thatcher," Ben said.

"I must tend to the cattle," Carlos said. "And the wagons." He touched a hand to his battered felt hat and turned his horse. *"Hasta luego,"* he said, and rode away toward the trees where the cattle were now coming through in large bunches. They could hear the drovers yelling and the cows bawling as they sighted the fresh grass.

"You forgot something, Carlos," John called after him. Carlos reined up the steeldust and turned the animal in a tight circle.

"What do I forget?"

John inclined his head toward Corny.

"Your new hand."

"Do you know anything about cows?" Carlos asked.

"Some," Corny said.

"Well, you gonna learn more. Come on."

Corny grinned.

"Thanks, Mr. Savage," he said as he rode off to catch up with Carlos, who was already putting his horse into a trot.

Ben and John watched the two ride off toward the edge of the plateau.

"I hope to hell you know what you're doing, John," Ben said.

"What are you worried about, Ben?"

"Aw, nothin' I guess. I just wondered if you could make a friend out of an enemy."

"Dave Cornwall's not a friend yet, Ben. He's another cowhand who has to prove himself."

"Corny ain't no cowhand."

"Maybe not yet, but Carlos will raise calluses on Corny's ass in the next day or two."

"That won't make that waddie a friend."

"Maybe not. But it might give him a profession and take down his fever."

"Fever? What fever?" Ben said.

"Gold fever," John said, and clucked to Gent. He headed toward the cabin before Ben could regain his senses.

More exactly, John rode toward Eva, who was still standing there, watching curly coated cattle swell their numbers in the green grass of their new home.

17

Eva walked away from the log where she and her mother had been sitting to meet John and Ben as they rode up.

"Hello, John," she said. "Ben."

"Good morning, Eva."

"I saw that man over there," she said. "Were you going to shoot him?"

"A warning shot. Over his head."

"Why didn't you?"

"Might have stampeded the cattle. Are you worried about him?"

"Who is he?"

"A bad man," Ben said. "Claim jumper."

Eva looked at John, whose eyes were fixed on her. She felt that fluttering of insect wings in her stomach, the flush of blood through her heart. His look softened and she was sure she saw his eyes brighten with light. She could almost feel his kiss on her lips, and her face burned with the wicked thought of it.

"I'll walk you to the house," she said, turning to go. "Do you want coffee?"

"Maybe just a taste," John said, and she turned her head at his words. Was there a hidden meaning in them? She was sure there was. She smiled and John smiled back at her.

He watched her walk to the cabin, the graceful way she stepped, the sculptured beauty of her buttocks, the way her dress clung to her shapely legs. He felt a sudden squeeze to his heart as if her hand had reached inside his chest. He took a quick breath to wipe out his lusty thoughts. Her long hair shone in the sun, and he had the urge to run the strands through his fingers, touch her cheek. He knew then that he had never had such feelings for a woman. He felt as if he had been struck by a bolt of lightning, an electric charge that sizzled his senses and made his skin tingle from his face to his toes.

Ben and John dismounted, while Eva entered the cabin. They tied their horses' reins to a hitching post that had been erected since their previous visit.

"Since when did you fire warnin' shots, Johnny?" Ben asked, a sarcastic twang in his voice.

"Since I gave up shooting humans for

sport," John said.

"I didn't know you did that, either," Ben retorted.

"Looking at you, Ben, I'm thinking of taking it up again."

Ben snorted and they walked to the cabin. The door was open, but John knocked on one of the wall logs.

"Come in, John," Eva called over the high pitch of her mother's voice.

Emma was railing at Whit, had him backed against the wall in the front room. John and Ben stopped just inside the entrance.

"You're not to go back with them, Whit," Emma screamed. "You haven't got sense enough to come in out of the rain."

"Ma, leave me alone," Whit said, his back to the wall, his eyes wide with shock.

Emma whirled to face John. She raised her arm and shook her index finger at him.

"You almost got my son killed," she said. "How dare you come into my house."

"Ma," Eva said. "Calm down."

"Calm down? My hair turned another shade of gray when I heard what almost happened to Whit last night. Those shots I heard. They were trying to kill my boy. I won't have it, you hear. I won't let you risk my son's life among that rabble down at the creek."

John held up both hands as if to ward off an attack by an angry mother.

"Hold on," he said in a calming tone of voice. "Whit was never in danger."

"What do you mean? Men came to your camp and shot at you or where they thought you were."

"Let me explain," John said, as Whit slid a few feet along the wall so his mother couldn't turn on him again.

"Seems to me you've got a lot of explaining to do, Mr. Savage."

"Sit down," he said, waving Emma to a chair. "Sit down and just listen."

There was now a commanding tone to his voice and Emma obeyed him, taking a chair at the table. Eva stood behind another chair, watching like a spectator at a prize fight, her eyes aglitter, her lips slightly parted.

John stood where he was and told her not only about the events of the night before, but also about how he and Ben had made dummy bedrolls and strung tins filled with pebbles across the trails as a warning system. Emma sat there, fuming, until the whole story came out and she felt a sense of calm.

"Ben and Whit were up in the mine, completely safe, and armed. None of those men would have been able to get at them.

Ben would have dropped the first one who poked his head above the ledge."

"Well, I just don't like to think about Whit being anywhere near such men as those."

"He's doing honest work and earning money for you and Eva," John said.

"I don't see no money," Emma said, a stubborn sheet of iron in her voice.

"It's not money yet," John said, pulling a small sack from under his belt. "It's gold dust and it spends the same as greenbacks."

He dropped the leather pouch on the table. It was tied with a thong through eyelets at the top of the sack.

"Go ahead," he told her. "Take a look. That's gold your son sweated for just to put food on your table. He's a hard worker."

Emma opened the pouch, peered inside. She opened it wider, and her eyes widened as well when she saw the glitter of gold dust. She pulled the thong tight and hefted the sack in her hand.

"How much is it worth?" she asked.

"Ben weighed it. Ben?"

"It's nigh to five ounces, Miz Blanchett," Ben said. "Worth sixteen dollars to the ounce most everywhere."

"Keep it someplace safe, Emma," John said. "When you go to town, you can buy yourself grub and pretties."

"When am I going to town?" she said, placing her hand over the pouch.

"Some of my men will be going to Denver for supplies in a week or so. You can ride in the wagon."

"You got a wagon?"

"We have three of them," Ben said, "if'n the wheels stay on."

"One of them's full of chuck," John said. "You'll eat well from now on, Emma."

"Well, this is certainly a surprise," she said. "I-I don't know what to say."

"Ma, don't say anything," Eva said. "Just leave Whit be. He's in good hands with John and Ben."

Emma looked over at Whit, who was still standing against the wall.

"I must say he's got color in his cheeks now. I guess that's a tan, like you and Ben have. He's filling out some, too. I guess I shouldn't worry so much."

"No, Ma," Whit said. "You shouldn't worry none at all. I'll be just fine."

"You like living down there on the creek, away from home and hearth?"

"Yes'm, I truly do."

"Well, maybe it'll make a man of you, Whit. I just don't want you to get shot or killed."

"I won't," he said, and came over to his

mother. "Don't you worry none, Ma."

Emma sighed.

"My, I'm forgetting my manners. John, would you and Ben like some coffee? Something to eat? I made a pie last night. Peach."

Both men shook their heads.

"I've got to help my men," John said. "Make sure those wagons get up here. I'll have them pull the chuck wagon up to the cabin here and make sure you get vittles and such. Just help yourself. The supply wagons will go where Ben and I want to build our house. And Carlos will put up a bunkhouse for the men. We'll be well away from you, Emma, so you'll have your privacy."

"Why, that's very considerate of you, John. And I welcome the vittles and what flour and sugar you might spare."

"There will be plenty," John said.

The two men touched fingers to their hat brims and walked outside.

Whit followed them.

"You stay with your mother and sister, Whit," John said. "I won't need you until tomorrow, maybe."

"I want to go with you and Ben, John."

"Best you stay here, Whit. Ben and I have some things to talk over."

"Are you going after them claim jumpers?"

"Now, sonny, don't you worry none about what John and I are going to do. Your ma needs to catch up on things besides what happened last night."

"Ben's right, Whit. I think your ma needs some comfort."

"Aw," Whit said, and Ben gave him a withering look.

"Go on, boy," Ben said, "and let us be."

Whit turned and slumped back into the cabin, kicking at dirt clods, like a boy being sent home from school before the final bell.

"He's a good kid, Ben," John said, as he grabbed the reins and unwrapped them from the hitch pole.

"He's a kid, all right, John. I don't know how good he is."

"Maybe if you quit riding him, you'd find out."

"I rode you when you was little more'n his age."

"Yeah, you did, and there were times when I wanted to bust a barrel stave across your head."

"Huh? I never knowed that."

"There's a lot you don't know, Ben. Young ones grow up to be men. And Whit's getting mighty close."

"That boy's a gangly whippersnapper with all the sense of a grasshopper and two hands full of thumbs."

The two mounted their horses and rode across the plain to where the cattle were still emerging from the trees in small clumps of four or five, then spreading out to find others of their kind nibbling on the shoots of grass.

"Patience is a virtue, Ben."

"Dognabit, John, I'm too old to raise a whelp like Whit Blanchett."

"Okay. Don't raise him. Just leave him be. I'll teach him how to pan for dust."

"Who taught you, John?"

John laughed. "You said I was born with the gift, Ben."

"Like hell. I taught you everything you know."

"Not everything, Ben."

Ben snorted, and they reached the trail just as one of the drovers was chasing the two milk cows and their calves onto the plain. Guernseys, their udders bulging with milk, their frisky calves bounding stiff-legged onto new ground, their tails wagging like puppies' tails.

Gasparo appeared ahead of the chuck wagon as it rumbled through the trees, swaying from side to side with its load.

John reined up Gent and pointed Gasparo toward the log cabin. Gasparo nodded and signaled the man on the wagon, a small wizened man with a long beard and a shock of gray hair, holding the reins. His cheek bulged out with a wad of chewing tobacco, and he spit out of the corner of his mouth as he made the turn.

"Where in hell did Carlos get him?" Ben asked.

"I don't know, but I hope to hell he can cook," John said.

"He sure can wrangle a chuck wagon, that's for sure."

The old man waved a thorny hand at Ben and John as the wagon trundled past with the clanging of pots and skillets and the rattle of wooden spoons and tin cups.

"Name's Dobbins," the toothless man yelled. "Ornery Dobbins from Cheyenne."

"Ornery?" Ben said, when the wagon had passed.

John smiled.

"Looks like he stole one of your names, Ben. I'd get after him for that."

Corny rode into sight ahead of one of the supply wagons. He waved to Ben and John.

"Looks like you got a new hand," Ben said.

"If the boot fits, I'm going to wear it,"

John said, and pointed out a direction for the supply wagon to take. He and Ben turned their horses and led the way across the wide valley that burned like green fire in the afternoon sun.

18

Harry Short was still limping, favoring his swollen knee. Al Krieger's hand was nearly back to normal. Most of the swelling had gone down, and there was only a purple bruise to remind him of John Savage's shot. He led the way down the game trail leading to the Savage mining claim. The trail was pocked with hoof marks where he and the others had ridden the night before.

As they neared the bend in the trail, Krieger held up his hand to halt Short.

"What's the matter?" Short whispered.

"Somethin' ain't right here."

Short limped up to stand beside Krieger.

"That just can't be," Short said.

The two men stared at the string of cans dangling above the path. They were strung together by strong twine between an aspen tree and a scrub pine growing out of the foot of the bluff.

"It can't be, but it damned sure is,"

Krieger whispered. A brief twinge of pain in his right hand made his spine stiffen. He muttered an unintelligible curse under his breath. It was plain to see that someone had repaired the alarm after the four of them had ridden through the Savage camp.

"Didn't we kill 'em all?" Short said, his voice pitched so low it was almost like a hiss of air.

"Maybe there was more'n two men workin' that claim. You see another bedroll?"

"I only saw the two. By the fire."

"Shit," Krieger said in a whisper.

The ensuing silence rippled with the gurgling flow of the creek off to their right. A light breeze flowed through the trees, rustling the aspen leaves, twisting them until some glowed green, while their undersides flickered with a pale white light. A jay screeched from a pine branch, and a chipmunk squealed a high-pitched whistle directed at the bird.

"Think we ought to go have a look-see?" Short asked.

"If we want to get our heads blown off, yeah," Krieger said.

"It's awful quiet. I don't hear no diggin' or sloshin'."

"They probably know we're here."

Krieger walked up to the strung twine,

careful not to touch or disturb the dangling cans. He stepped along the length of the string from tree to tree. He bent over, studied the ground.

There were horse tracks, but the boot prints covered some of those. It was plain to see that men had repaired the alarm after Krieger and his men had ridden through the mining camp.

"I count four sets of boot tracks here," he said when he was finished.

"I thought they was only two on this claim," Short said.

"There was that kid. Whit something."

"That makes three."

"Four boot tracks," Krieger said. "I counted 'em twice."

"Are you thinkin' what I'm thinkin', Al?"

Krieger didn't answer. He just stared at Short with narrowed eyes as if mulling the question over in his mind. His face was like stone. No expression at all. Just hard.

Short looked up at the bluff, and into the trees. He stared at the string of tin cans, the sag of the yellowish twine, felt the tug of the breeze at his hat brim. A quail piped in the distance, a lonesome sound in the unearthly silence.

"They're bein' mighty quiet, Al."

"Yeah, like they're expectin' us. I'm wonderin' now if we killed Corny. And, if we did, maybe they found him.

"Or maybe we didn't kill Corny, neither. Shortie, I don't like none of this. The way it's shapin' up, I think we made a hell of a mistake."

"Hell, it was dark, Al."

"I think we ought to check. Make sure."

"How?"

"You want to walk up to their camp and make sure? I'll cover you."

Short looked as if Krieger had punched him in the gut. He shook his head.

"I ain't goin' no further'n this, Al. You want to check, you go."

"All right. I'll look around that campfire they had burnin', and then we'll go find where Corny had that lean-to, see if he's lyin' bloody and dead under all them limbs."

"Watch your step, Al."

Krieger stepped over the twine, careful not to rattle any of the cans. He disappeared around a bend in the bluff.

Short felt his skin crawl with invisible lice. He didn't like to think of what they had done to Corny, but that was Thatcher's idea, and his order. Thatcher thought too much sometimes. So did Ferguson. But now he wondered if they had not thought enough. Those cans were hanging back up

179

across their path and it wasn't no ghost what put 'em there.

Krieger returned in a few minutes, walking natural, making noise with his boots.

"Well, are they dead?" Short asked as Krieger stepped over the twine. He didn't rattle any cans, but he wasn't as careful as he had been.

"Not a speck of blood, and they was two piles of rocks where we thought them two was sleepin' and a horse blanket shot full of holes."

"Christ," Short breathed.

"Let's cross the creek and find that shot-up lean-to of Corny's."

"Jesus, Al, ain't it enough that we didn't kill Savage and that Russell feller?"

"Follow me, Harry," Krieger said.

The two men waded across the creek and entered the woods. They found the lean-to, or what was left of it. Krieger lifted a spruce bough and examined the ground. Short stood by, nervously looking all around, his rifle held across his chest with both hands.

"Any blood?" Short asked. "You see any blood under there?"

"Nary a drop."

"So, we didn't kill Corny, neither," Short said, his voice quivering with a nameless fear.

"Harry," Krieger whispered, "I think we ought to hightail it back to camp and tell Thatcher. Somethin' ain't right here."

"Maybe Pete found out something up past them bluffs. Ferguson wanted him to find out what all the yellin' and cattle bawlin' was about."

"Yeah, he reckons Savage might have run some cattle up on that tabletop. I only saw it once, but it was a lot of grassland."

"Well, Ferguson wants to know everything, and he doesn't know shit, you ask me."

"Walt's a smart man. So is Thatcher."

"He picked a poor spot to prospect."

"That should have been a good place to dig for gold," Krieger said.

"Yeah, but it wasn't."

"Let's go back. This place is too damned spooky for me."

"Thatcher won't like it none."

"Then, let him go on the scout. This place gives me the pure willies. Same as that empty camp."

"Me, too," Short said, hefting the heavy Henry rifle and shifting it to his other hand.

Krieger turned around, swinging the barrel of his rifle against a low-hanging pine branch. The sound made both men jump.

19

Thatcher was in a bad mood. After Krieger and Short had left camp on their mission, he slipped on a slimy rock in the creek and fell in. He twisted his ankle and was soaking wet when he crawled out. His hat floated downstream.

"Grab my hat, Walt. I paid a sawbuck for that Stetson."

Ferguson ran down to where the hat floated and waded in, but the hat bounced off a rock and skittered away on the current and drifted out of sight.

"Missed it," Ferguson said.

Thatcher unlaced his boot and pulled off his sock. He began massaging his ankle as Ferguson walked back, his pants soaked, his boots waterlogged. They squished with every step.

"I got another one, somewhere," Thatcher said.

"Twist your ankle?"

"No, I just like to rub my foot every six months or so. What the hell do you think?"

"Don't get short with me, Lem. You're the one who thought he could walk on water."

"You're not only a poor hat fetcher, Walt, you got a smart mouth."

"Better'n havin' a dumb one like Corny."

"The less you mention Corny's name, the better off we'll all be," Thatcher said, wincing as he put his foot down. His ankle was turning red and was beginning to swell.

Ferguson tightened down on his emotions, keeping them under his hat so he would not vent his anger at Thatcher, an anger that had been building for some time. It was Thatcher who had picked out this place as a likely claim, and he was no geologist. He was just a greedy man with gold fever, as far as Ferguson could tell. This stretch of creek had looked promising because it was shallow, and they had panned a little dust in those days before they filed their claim. But, as they had found out, it was a poor place to pan or dig for gold. The spring runoff had depleted most of the dust that had lain in the creek bottom for untold years. They had dug out roots along the banks and found no nuggets and only a smattering of dust. The placers were not producing anything but black sand and the men were bickering privately, among themselves.

To himself, Ferguson thought, "I hope your ankle swells up and busts open like a muskmelon."

To Thatcher, he said: "Al and Harry ought to have been back by now. They didn't take no food with 'em and it's way past noon."

"Hell, in these damned mountains, it's almost sundown," Thatcher said, and pulled on a wet sock. The cool cloth felt good on his ankle, but he was not ready for the soggy boot yet. He crawled to the edge of the creek and stuck his sore foot into the stream. Ferguson picked up a pan and squatted by the creek, dug the edge into the water, and scooped up sand and water. He began to shake and tilt the pan until the muddy water was swirling. Every so often, he sloshed water out until there was only a small amount swirling around, shifting the sands, spilling out extra gravel.

"I hear 'em comin'," Thatcher said.

Ferguson couldn't hear from the noise of his panning. He stopped swirling the water and listened. He turned to face the south, set down the pan, and put his hand on the butt of his .44 Remington. A jay screamed in the aspens, squawked at the approaching men.

"Is that them?" Thatcher asked. He was not packing iron, and the cool water took the heat out of his ankle.

"I can't tell. But someone's sure comin' and makin' a lot of noise."

"Hello, the camp," Krieger called as he hove into view, brushing through aspen branches. Behind him came Short, his tanned face scrunched into a scowl. His rifle rested on his right shoulder. He was carrying something in his left hand. Something wet and dripping.

"Yeah, Al," Thatcher yelled back, "you better have some good tidings for me."

"I got tidings, all right, Lem. But they ain't good."

Thatcher jerked his socked foot out of the water and scooted his butt farther up on the bank.

"This your hat, Lem?" Short said, holding up the soggy felt hat. "Found it down the creek a ways."

"Toss it to me, Harry," Thatcher said. He caught it with both hands, rolled it up, and wrung it out. Then he unfolded the soggy mass and put it on his head. Krieger stared down at him as he put the butt of his Henry on the ground next to his leg. Harry glared up at him.

"You want to hear it all, Lem?" Krieger

said, stuffing a wad of tobacco in his mouth.

"Spill it, Al. You might as well keep on ruinin' my day."

"Sorry about your hat, Lem," Harry said, a sheepish look on his face. "What's wrong with your foot?"

"You tryin' to change the subject, Harry?"

"Nope, I just noticed you was soakin' that foot in the creek and you ain't got a boot on it."

"Well, what did you notice at the Savage diggings? You gonna tell me, Al, or do I have to pry it out of you with a crowbar?"

Krieger told them about the two sets of rocks where they thought bedrolls were, the lack of blood on the ground, and the camp being deserted.

"And that ain't all," Short said as he leaned his rifle against a rock.

Krieger chewed the chunk of tobacco and spit a stream of brown juice onto a bare rock.

"We checked that lean-to of Corny's," Krieger said. "It was flattened like a griddle cake."

"And?" Thatcher urged.

"And no blood, no Corny, no nothin'," Krieger said.

"Shit fire," Thatcher said.

"Sorry, Boss," Krieger said. "Looks like

Savage outfoxed us."

"I'm glad you said 'us,' Al," Thatcher said, a sarcastic snarl to his tone. "We was all buffaloed."

"Yeah."

Ferguson walked over.

"No sign of Savage or Corny?" he said, looking at Krieger.

Krieger shook his head. "I saw four sets of boot tracks coverin' up our horse tracks. Three big ones and a smaller one."

"A smaller one?" Thatcher said, wincing as he moved his injured foot.

"Maybe that kid's with 'em. That Blanchett boy what we whupped."

"So, there's four of them now, instead of two," Ferguson said. He threw the words in Thatcher's face with a look of disgust. "That sure cuts down the odds some, Al."

"What in hell do you know about odds, Walt? You couldn't win a horse race or a hand of poker when we was in Dodge City."

"Seems to me you weren't doin' none too good, neither, Al," Ferguson said.

He was from Clitherall, Minnesota, and he had met up with Thatcher in Dodge City, Kansas, almost a year ago, when both were down on their luck. Thatcher hailed from someplace in Illinois or Ohio, had run away from home, worked as a swamper in saloons,

187

took up the owlhoot trail robbing travelers and pilgrims, wound up in Dodge City where the money flowed like water and was just as slippery.

"I got to think," Thatcher said. "Give me a chaw of that tobacco, Al."

Krieger reached into his pocket and pulled out a plug, tossed it down to Thatcher, who bit off a chew and tossed it back.

"Somebody help me get up," he said, raising one of his arms. Short pulled him to his feet. He stood there like a wounded crane, one leg straight, the other cocked above the ground.

Ferguson looked off to the north, squinted his eyes.

"Let's see what Pete has to say," he said. "Here he comes."

All the men looked around and saw Pete Rosset riding down a slope, leaning back in the saddle, tugging on his reins to keep his horse from running out from under him. He made the bottom and headed their way.

The sun had drifted over the bluffs and the light was slanted, glinting off the tops of pines and burnishing the aspen leaves that twisted like dancers in the soft breeze of afternoon. The creek was turning dark as shadows dusted its ripples.

Rosset didn't seem anxious to ride up, and

his progress was painfully slow to watch. Thatcher spit out tobacco juice and breathed through his nostrils.

"You're takin' your sweet time, Pete," Krieger called. "Ain't your horse got any git-up in him?"

"We're both of us tired as hell, Al," Rosset said, wiping sweat from his forehead. "It's a long hard way up to that tabletop from here."

"Well, get your ass over here and tell me what you saw. Settlers?"

Rosset rode up and slumped over, his hands resting on his saddle horn. He slipped his boots out of the stirrups and stretched his legs.

"They's a whole bunch of Messicans up there," he said to Thatcher. "They was bringin' in beeves and wagons. They's a cabin up there and folks livin' in it. Hell, they got 'em a chuck wagon and supply wagons stacked with lumber and barrels. Saw Corny, too."

"What?" Thatcher said.

"Yep, Corny was there and I think he saw me. One feller throwed down on me, but he didn't shoot. Young feller with what looked like a Winchester '73."

"Savage," Krieger said. "I'd bet money on it."

"Corny on a horse?" Thatcher asked.

"Yep, a horse I never seen before. There was that kid with 'em, too."

"You count head?" Ferguson asked.

"Didn't have time. More'n fifty head of whitefaces, but they was still comin' onto the tabletop when I lit a shuck."

"What in hell's that bastard up to?" Thatcher said. It was a rhetorical question. He didn't expect an answer.

"Seems like he's plannin' to stay," Ferguson said.

"Hell, he's likely to build him a city up there. I ain't seen so many Messicans since we left Denver," Rosset said.

"This changes everything," Ferguson said.

"It don't change nothin'," Thatcher retorted. "I still aim to put that bastard's lamp out and jump his claim. I didn't come up here to watch some other sonofabitch get rich."

"You gonna do this by yourself, Lem?" Ferguson said, his tone etched with acid, the kind that drips on a man's brain and poisons his whole body.

"It can be done, Walt. We just need to put our heads together. Come up with a plan."

Rosset swung down out of the saddle. He slipped his canteen from his saddle horn, pulled the cork, and drank. Krieger shifted uncomfortably on his feet. Short spit a wad of tobacco down at his feet, looking as if he wanted to be as far away as he could get by just wishing.

"A plan, Lem?" Ferguson said. "As good as the last one? As good as the paper our claims are written on?"

The acid was thick as molasses.

"You keep on, Walt, and see where you get."

"You threatenin' me, Lem?"

"Not yet, Walt. You'll know when I do."

The two men glared at each other. Rosset cleared his throat and started to loosen his saddle cinch. He rubbed the side of his face. Krieger's eyes glittered in the dying light as if there were a flame building inside him, a bloodlust such as a man brought to a prize fight.

"It ain't the end of the world," Short said, finally. "Maybe that Savage feller is a-goin' to give up prospectin' and take to cattle ranchin'."

Thatcher stared at Short as if the man had lost his mind or gotten into the whiskey stores.

"Yeah, Harry," Ferguson said, "and maybe pigs got wings and can fly."

"Harry's right," Thatcher said. "We still got some moves left. We'll sleep on it tonight and talk in the morning. Maybe drink a little whiskey tonight to wash out the bad taste in our mouths."

Ferguson walked away in disgust, turning his back on Thatcher.

Whiskey wasn't going to solve a damned thing, Ferguson thought. But already, his mouth was filling up with saliva just thinking about it. That was Thatcher's way, had been back in Dodge. When times got tough, it was time for a man to pour himself a stiff drink of Old Taylor.

But he knew damned well that drinking whiskey with Lem Thatcher wouldn't solve a damned thing.

20

John watched as Ornery Dobbins guided his team of two horses up to the cabin and deftly maneuvered the chuck wagon into the spot John had designated beforehand. Dobbins set the brake as Eva and Emma ran up to the wagon, their eyes wide at the sight of such a marvel.

"Set it up, Ornery," John said as he rode up, "and get to cooking. There are a lot of mouths to feed."

Dobbins cocked his head, pushed his derby hat back an inch, and, gimlet-eyed, stared at John as if he were a weevil creeping into his flour bin.

"I can feed four or forty, mister. You got any water up here? I need helpers. I can do the cookin' all right, as far as taste goes, but I ain't no magician and I only have two hands."

Before John could answer, Emma stepped forward.

"My daughter and I will be glad to help," she said.

"Can you peel taters, slice onions, prepare sugar beets?"

"Yes, we can, sir."

Dobbins climbed down from the seat and danced a little jig in front of the two women, lifting his derby as he circled them, pumping it up and down like a vaudeville performer.

"Only one cook here, ladies. Too many spoil the broth, ye know. But you can peel and slice and chop if you're willin', and I'll cook you a feast that will stick to your ribs like glue."

Eva squealed with delight at Dobbins's antics, and as she jumped up and down, her pigtails flogged her back like silken whips. Emma smiled and tapped her feet in time to Dobbins's steps.

John shook his head and rode off toward the supply wagons.

"We have water," Emma was saying. "Springwater, and we can fetch all you need, sir."

"Name's Ornery, ma'am. Ornery Dobbins."

"Ornery? That's an odd name."

"Not as odd as what my real moniker is, pretty lady."

Emma blushed.

"And what, may I ask, is your real name, Mr. Dobbins?"

"Why, that's a secret I keep to myself and you look most becoming when you blush, you nameless beauty of a woman."

"My name's Emma. Emma Blanchett. And this is my daughter Eva."

"Pleased to meet you, Ornery," Eva said, and curtsied, pulling her dress out to her sides like a fan.

"The pleasure is all mine, Miss Eva," Dobbins said. "You are a most winsome lass yourself. Now, will you both step up and show me your hands? Palms up, if you please."

Emma and Eva walked over to Dobbins and held out their hands. He lifted Emma's hands and turned them over, then moved to Eva. He examined her hands, as well, and then stepped back.

"You both have lovely hands, and I see they are not strangers to work. From the looks of them, I would say you have scrubbed, washed, hammered, and sawed. Now, I'd like one of you to peel ten pounds of potatoes, and the other to chop up a half dozen onions, and can we get about ten gallons of water?"

"Whit," Emma called as she turned to

look at the cabin. "Come here."

Whit came running, and Dobbins handed him a large blackened kettle.

"Would you be so kind as to fill this kettle, young man, a hand span below the rim, if you please."

"Yes, sir," Whit said as he took the kettle from Dobbins. He ran off into the woods and disappeared.

"Now, then," Dobbins said. "Taters and onions for my stew." And he walked to the back of the chuck wagon, dropped the tailgate, reached in, and grabbed two sacks. As the women crowded up to him, he laid out cutting boards and knives, along with a battered bucket that he set on the ground.

"I'll do the potatoes, Eva, while you peel and chop up the onions."

"Oh, dear," Eva said. "I am surely going to cry."

Dobbins laughed and walked to a cupboard on the side of the wagon, where he retrieved a small shovel. He began to dig a pit and lined it with stones. When Whit returned, he told him to bring plenty of kindling wood and logs cut to a length of two and a half feet each. He hummed to himself as he set up a sideboard with salt, pepper, and other condiments, humming a merry little tune that put the women in a good mood as they peeled and chopped and watched the bucket fill up.

The sun sank slowly beyond the distant peaks, flaming the string of clouds with peach and salmon, shooting rays through them in a wide fan that seemed to proclaim the glory of either the heavens or the western sky, depending on a person's preference. Twilight crept through the pine forest, as the sun gilded the trees' green crowns, and hushed the jays and the crows.

Some of the cattle were lining the banks of the two spring-fed streams that coursed through the plateau, while others were scattered over several acres, nibbling grass. John rode through their long shadows, admiring them with a feeling of warm contentment. The stock seemed at home, and that gave him much pleasure. There were bulls among the herd, and some had already gathered their harems around them, watching over them with wary eyes on the younger bulls.

"Get those wagon sheets out and carry them up to the house," John told Pepito. "Lay them out on the flattest place you can find in front of that cabin."

"We will have the music and the dancing?" Pepito said.

"You bet your boots, Pepito."

Pepito grinned and went back to unloading a wagon of its lumber and tools. The other supply wagon was nearly empty, the lumber stacked neatly on a large tarpaulin sheet. Gasparo and Corny were pulling the last of the two-by-fours from the wagon bed. A pair of guitar cases lay nearby, alongside a fiddle case.

"You doing all right, Corny?" John asked.

"It feels good to be doing some honest work for a change," he said.

"There's nothing dishonest about gold panning," John said.

"That depends."

"Depends on what?"

"On where you're panning and who you're panning with," Corny said.

"I see your point," John said. "Gasparo, don't forget the wagon sheets."

"We will carry them up to the cabin, John. Do not worry."

"Then I want you and Corny here to put up a small corral near the cabin. For the milk cows and their calves. Can you do that? Just put up a quick pole corral."

"I can do that, John. There is much timber for such a corral."

"I will tell Renaldo to get some axes," John said, and rode off toward the cabin, through the long shadows of late afternoon stretching from the grazing cattle and the tall trees that bordered the plateau. He looked at the fiery sky and knew they would have good weather on the morrow, and, with luck, a starry night and a moon to light the entire tabletop and keep the wolves at bay.

Gasparo looked across the pasture and pointed. John saw a man leading two Guernsey cows and their calves.

"Renaldo brings the cows," Gasparo said. "We will have milk in the morning."

"I'll show him where to take them," John said, and rode off at a fast trot.

Renaldo Alicante sat in a small spruce grove, holding the two ropes that held the cows as they grazed in place. He was waiting for orders from either Carlos or John. He waved to John as he rode up.

"*Hola,* Renaldo," John said.

"Will you take one of the ropes, John?" Renaldo said as he rode up to John. "My hand is sore from holding them."

"Sure." John leaned down and took a rope from Renaldo, who flexed his hand to restore circulation.

"This is a good place," Renaldo said. "Much grass. Much land."

"Yes," John said. "To me it is Eden."

"Ah. To me it is Argentina." Renaldo had lived in Argentina for many years, learned about cattle from the *gauchos.* He was a good *vaquero.*

John looked up at the sky to the west. It would be dark soon and there was much to do. The sun was slipping down behind the most distant peaks, and many of the purple clouds were dusky, the light draining from them like sand through a sieve. The shadows beneath the trees had thickened to dark puddles, and the treetops were gradually fading into the faint bronze color of old tintypes.

"Tie these cows up, Renaldo," John said, handing him his rope. "Pick a spot for a corral. Tonight, you'd better lay your bedroll close by. The wolves might find those calves mighty tempting."

Renaldo got to his feet. The calves were staying close to their mothers, but were still frisky. They chased each other in between bumps to their mother's udders, and wagged their short tails at each new discovery in their new home.

"Keep your pistol close tonight after you go to bed," said John.

He left Renaldo and went looking for Ben and Carlos. Dobbins had a fire going, and John's stomach twisted in hunger as he rode into the gathering twilight, across the plain, and into the hush of early evening. Shadows moved around the cook fire like actors on a stage, and he heard the crinkle of Eva's laughter, the lilting brogue of Dobbins as he voiced an Irish ditty, while some of the cows moaned low in their throats as they began to bed down.

He saw the men carrying the wagon sheets across the grassy plateau, and the darkness beyond where the world had disappeared and nothing was visible. A pair of quail whirred by like oversized insects and glided into the trees along the edge of the grassland, and he heard the first querulous ribbon of fluting notes from the throat of an owl.

Ben loomed out of the gloaming, riding toward the cabin.

"Where's Carlos?" John asked.

"Over at the north creek," Ben said. "One of the cows stirred up a rattler and got bit in the leg."

"Let's find him, Ben, before it's full dark."

"It's full dark over yonder now, John. I couldn't see my hand in front of my face."

"All right, we'll find him, anyway."

"You can see in the dark, Johnny?"

"About as well as you can, Ben. But we'll know where Carlos is when we hear him cussing in Spanish."

Ben laughed.

"He'd be doin' that, all right," Ben said,

and they rode to the creek, listening for the liquid sound of Spanish invective, two shadows on horseback as the blue sky blackened and the first stars began to sparkle in the blackness above them.

21

Pepito tackled the convulsing steer, grabbing one of its hind legs as it thrashed the brush and kicked at him. Carlos dove for its neck, grabbed its left horn, and wrestled it to the ground. The horn dug into the dirt as the animal crashed down. Juanito grabbed another leg and pulled it toward the other. The cow kicked, and its sharp hoof struck Juanito in the groin. He cried out and doubled over in pain, his testicles swelling from the blow.

"Hold him," Carlos said in Spanish.

Carlos twisted the steer's head, while putting some of his weight on its neck in a bulldogging maneuver.

"Ay de mi, no puedo," Pepito cried as the steer pulled its leg free and kicked Pepito in the stomach while it twisted its lower body away from Carlos, trying to get away. The animal was breathing hard, trying to twist its head and lift it to smash its tormentor

with a vicious sweep of its horn.

Carlos groaned as he fought to keep the steer's head twisted, but the burly animal shifted its body and got its hind legs under it. Still, Carlos hung on.

Pepito reached out and grabbed a rear hock, but the steer kicked and the foot flew out of Pepito's grasp.

"*Andale,* Pepito," Carlos yelled. "Hurry."

Pepito scrambled to his feet as the darkness deepened. He rushed the steer and butted it in the flank with his head, pushed on its hind quarters with both hands. The animal staggered and toppled over onto its rump.

The steer shook its head, trying to break Carlos's grip, but Carlos held on, his boots digging furrows into the ground as he pushed and pushed.

John heard the scuffle as he rode up, and saw the dark shapes squirming on the ground.

He watched as the two men wrestled with the steer. They turned like a pinwheel on the ground as the heavy animal fought to free itself.

"*Mi cuchillo,*" Carlos grunted. "My knife."

John jumped from the saddle and ran over to him, drawing his knife.

"*Corta la garganta,*" Carlos said in Spanish.

John understood him. "Cut his throat."

He knelt down, grabbed the free horn, and pulled the steer's head back, so far back he heard something crack. Then he slashed the blade of his knife across the animal's throat, cutting through hide and sinew, clear to the windpipe. Blood gushed from the open wound, drenching John's hand and knife.

Pepito wrapped his arms around both hind legs, pinning the steer's rump to the ground. The steer twisted in its death throes, kicked both hind legs in a quivering last spasm.

Carlos let out a breath as the steer's craggy head relaxed with a final quiver, the mouth open, the tongue lolling to one side.

Carlos sat up, slumped over, panting. Pepito loosened his grip on the legs, rolled to his side, and lay there, gasping.

"This is a hell of a way to put meat on the table," John said.

Neither man answered as both struggled for breath.

John wiped the blade of his knife on his trousers and slipped it back in its sheath.

He sat there, watching the two men, listening to their labored breathing. The steer lay still; blood pooled up under its neck and head, a black mass in the darkness. Starlight sprinkled its silvery dust on the three men, their faces in shadow, smelling of sweat and cow, of churned-up earth and the reek of death.

"The snake," Carlos panted. "The snake, he bite the steer. In the leg."

"Might have saved him," John said.

Carlos shook his head.

"No, the poison, she go in deep. The snake bite three, four times, I think."

"That is so," Pepito said. "Five times, I think. In the legs, in the stomach. The cow was dying."

"Well, let's get it butchered and hung up to cure," John said. "Dobbins will be happy."

"I killed the snake," Carlos said. "It had many rattles. I smashed its head with a rock."

"Well, we can throw the snake in the stew, too."

Pepito made a sound of disgust in his throat.

"I have eaten snake," Carlos said. "It tastes like the legs of a frog."

"I thought it tasted like chicken," John said.

Pepito made another sound.

"It tastes like pig," he said in Spanish, then gurgled again as if he were going to vomit.

There were a few moments when the men

did not talk, but only listened to the lyrical flow of the meandering creek and breathed deeply of the night air. In the distance, they heard fluttering scraps of laughter floating down to them from the cabin, and the whisper of wings as an owl flapped its wings to climb to a higher altitude as it hunted along the stream.

"Carlos, I want us to stand guard tonight. After supper. Two shifts, two men."

"Do you expect trouble, *jefe?*"

"No. But I want to make sure. I want your men to walk, not ride, and listen."

"Listen for what?"

"Anything that doesn't sound right. Horses, men."

"Why do we walk? There is much land here."

"If your men were on horses, they would be easy targets. So, they walk."

"Two men only?"

"Sound carries far at night in this thin air. Two men would not make much noise and they could hear if men on horseback came into this wide valley."

"You tell me more, John. There is nothing to hear up here except the wolves, the owls, and the coyotes. Do you have fear that men will come here in the night?"

"Down on that creek where Ben and I

have our claim are some men I don't trust. One of them was up here today. I just want to make sure the others don't pay us a visit during the night."

"How many men?"

"I do not know. Four, at least."

"These are bad men?"

"These are very bad men, Carlos."

"And, if we see them, do we shoot them?"

"You ask a good question. I don't want you to fight my fight. But I would like to know if these men come up here."

"And you will shoot them?"

"If it comes to that."

"Ahh, and you think that it will, John."

"They tried to kill us last night."

"Oh, I see."

"I just want to make sure nobody gets hurt."

"The women," Carlos said.

Pepito scooted closer so he could hear every word Carlos and John were saying.

"The women, the boy, you, and your men," said John.

"Are they rustlers of the cattle, these men?"

"I don't think they know one end of a cow from the other, Carlos. They are claim jumpers. They have gold fever. Only they want my gold."

208

"Ah, then, we kill them," Pepito said.

"I'm not asking you to do that, Pepito."

"You do not like killing, then," Pepito said.

"No, I do not like to kill a man."

"But you have killed many. That is what they say."

"Pepito," Carlos said, "be silent. You talk too much."

"It is hard to kill a man," John said, rising to his feet. "And I would not ask you to do this. Just let me know if any of those men show up, and I'll take care of them."

"You will kill them," Pepito insisted. He was like a child sitting in class. He wanted to learn. He was very eager to learn.

"I hope not," John said.

"I will have the men watch and listen," Carlos said.

"Butcher this steer and bring it up to the chuck wagon. Get yourselves some grub. Is Dobbins a good cook?"

"Oh, he is a very good cook," Carlos said. "If he likes you."

Pepito and Carlos laughed.

"And if he does not?"

"You may find a scorpion in your soup," Pepito said.

"A living scorpion," Carlos added.

"I will see you two at supper," John said. "Load the meat in one of the wagons and bring it up."

Ben walked out to meet John when he rode up to the cabin. The cook fire blazed high and gilded his silhouette while leaving his face and features in shadow.

"Smells good," John said.

"Beef stew, John."

"My stomach's brushing up against my backbone."

"Got a question for you. Do we unsaddle and stay up here or go back to the mine?"

"Good question," John said as he swung down out of the saddle. "What do you think we should do?"

"We ride back down to the creek in the dark and we risk a horse breaking a leg. And we'd also be sleepin' in a cold black cave when we've got a fire here and millions of stars for a ceiling."

The two men walked to where the other horses were hobbled. Conversation flowed around the cook fire. Eva waved to John and smiled. He waved back and smiled, too. Emma was stirring the large cook pot under Ornery's supervision. Both were wearing aprons smeared with grease and vegetable juices. Their faces were daubed with orange light and flickering shadows.

"My hunch is that we're better off staying up here for the night," John said. "Thatcher might wreck our camp, but I doubt it. If we're not there, he won't have anything to shoot at."

Ben chuckled.

"I wonder if he knows how we fooled him by now," Ben said.

"Maybe. If he thought we were all dead, he might have jumped our claim. If he sent a man or two to bury us, he's going to be wondering what kind of fool he is."

"And he'll be madder'n a hornet by now."

"That's to our benefit," John said.

"Oh? You want him mad?"

"A man who's blind mad can't think too straight, Ben."

John ground-tied Gent and patted his withers.

"You going to leave him saddled?"

"Might need him during the night. Carlos will have men on guard."

"You think Thatcher will come up here tonight?"

"No, but with him, it's like having a rattlesnake in the picnic basket. The cover looks all right, a little checkered cloth, maybe, but there's still that snake inside, all coiled up, ready to strike."

"I see what you mean, John. I'll keep Rusher under saddle tonight."

The two men walked over to the cook fire.

Eva walked out to meet them.

"Hungry, John?" she said, flashing a smile that stung John's heart.

"I could eat the south end of a north-bound horse."

She laughed.

"Lucky you. It's beef in the pot. Did you ever go to a pie social?"

John cocked his head, puzzled.

"No, I don't believe so."

"Our church used to have them. The women baked pies and the men bid money on them. If a man bought a pie from a girl or a woman, he got to sit down and eat the pie with her."

"Are you suggesting . . ."

"I'd like to bring you your plate and have supper with you, John. That's what I'm suggesting."

"Do I have to buy my supper?"

"No, of course not."

"Then, I'd like to have supper with you."

"I guess I'll eat by myself," Ben said.

"Or with my mother," Eva said.

Ben grinned.

"You know, gal, that's the best offer I've had all day. I been to some pie socials. Mighty nice. I'll ask Emma if she'll sup with me."

Ben walked off as Eva and John laughed.

She took his arm in hers and walked, not toward the firelight, but off into the dark shadows of the trees. He felt her warmth and smelled her perfume. She smelled of flowers and earth, as well, and when she covered his hand with hers, he felt his legs go weak.

Neither of them noticed Whit watching them, a curious expression on his face. His eyes narrowed to black slits, and his mouth was bent in a harsh frown.

Ben saw the look on Whit's face, but did not say anything. It was something he would mull over, though, and something he would remember.

He knew jealousy when he saw it, and it was a condition that was ugly and a thing to be feared.

22

Eva pulled John under the branches of a tall pine, placed both hands on his chest. He felt wet and sticky, and she jerked her hands away in surprise.

"Ooooh," she said, turning one of her hands over to catch the light on her palm.

Her hand was smeared with blood.

"Are you hurt?" she asked.

"No, Eva." He took her hands and rubbed the palms on his dry sleeve. "We butchered a steer a while ago."

"You scared me," she said.

"I didn't mean to."

He released her hands and she stepped in close again. She looked up at him. He took a bandanna out of his back pocket, wiped his shirtfront, offered it to Eva. She wiped her hands and handed the kerchief back to John.

"I hope you don't think I'm too bold," she purred, her voice soft and silky.

"How bold do you think you are?"

"Too bold for Ma, maybe."

"Do you have to get her permission to be with a man?"

"No. But I think Ma has eyes for you, same as me."

"Same as I," he said, a smile crinkling on his mouth.

"What?"

"Grammar, Eva."

"Oh, that. Yes, I studied grammar in school. Are you going to keep correcting me?"

"I'm not your teacher, Eva."

He leaned down and kissed her with a gentleness that sent her blood racing. His kiss felt like velvet. It was not as she had expected, but then she had never kissed a man before. She would have thought men would be rougher with their kisses. This was like a mother's soft kiss, but more thrilling, more electrifying.

"I wish you would be," she said when he raised his head.

"What?"

"Be my teacher." There was a wickedness in her voice that would have shocked her mother, and that surprised her.

"How old are you, Eva?"

"I'm almost twenty. Why?"

"I'm a little older than you. Not much. But wouldn't you rather be with someone close to your own age?"

"I'd rather be with you, John. You can't be much older than me."

He wasn't, he thought. Not in years, perhaps, counting birthdays. But in experience. The things he had done and the things that had been done to him had hardened something inside him, had aged him in other ways. He felt very much older than she. Except now. She made him feel young. As young as she. It was a good feeling, and he didn't want to lose it or have it taken away. And he didn't want to take her young age away from her, either.

He kissed her again, harder this time, and she went limp in his arms. She felt as if all the blood had gone out of her brain and into her pounding heart.

"Mmmm," she murmured. "So nice. So sweet."

"You don't need lessons in kissing, Eva."

"Oh, I think I do. I never kissed a man before. Or a boy, even."

"Never?"

"Never," she said. "But when I first saw you, John, I wanted to spoon."

"Spoon?"

"You know, hold your hands. Have you

216

cuddle me. Didn't you? When you saw me, I mean."

"Well, I don't think I thought that far."

"Huh?"

"Your eyes said something to me, Eva. I admit that. Stirred something inside me."

"What? Do you know?"

He lowered his head and smelled her hair. He reached behind her and grabbed her pigtails, rubbed their soft strands.

"A kind of longing, I guess. When my folks were killed, and my little sister, I grew up fast, but I was still a boy. Only I never had a boyhood. I went from boy to man real quick."

"That's awful," she said.

"You don't miss what you never had," he said.

"I guess I know what you mean. I don't think I had much of a girlhood myself. And Pa scared me. He was awful mean and he-he — well, I can't talk about that. I won't talk about him no more."

"Eva," he said, and his voice trailed off. He was full of tangled feelings and he wasn't sure that he could express himself without sticking his foot in his mouth.

"What?" she said, her voice a whisper full of promise.

"I don't know. I-I guess you've got me sort

of tongue-tied."

She laughed, low in her throat, and it was like music to his ears.

"You don't really have to say anything, John. I'm happy just being with you. I wish we . . ."

"Wish we could what?"

"It's not my place," she said, and dipped her head in a display of sudden shyness. "I mean, I hope I'll see more of you than I have."

He drew in a deep breath, let it out slow through his nostrils.

Eva made him feel lightheaded and light-footed, as if he were standing on air and not on the ground. He had never met anyone like her. She was so beautiful and she stirred deep feelings within him, feelings that were new and strange to him.

"I hope we can see more of each other, Eva. I want to know all I can about you. And I want you to know all about me."

"Oh, yes," she said. "Let's meet and spoon, walk in the moonlight, wade in the creek, sit and talk, and . . ."

He knew what she meant. She was opening up a world to him, a world he had never known. He wanted to do all those things with her, and more. Much more.

They kissed again, and this time, he did

not take his lips away, but held her tight against him, feeling the softness of her yielding breasts and the heat of her thighs pressing against his. His eyes were closed and he never wanted to open them again, never wanted to let the world they had just then go away.

There was another world, he knew, and he did not want to return to it. Not now, not for a long time. He wished they could just ride off together and find some peaceful valley where they could live and love and lock themselves away from all the cares and troubles of civilization.

"Come and get it," Ornery yelled, and clanged an iron triangle that pealed through the valley and up into the mountains.

John broke the kiss and breathed.

"Oh, do we have to?" she said.

He laughed.

"There is another world," he said. "And we have to eat."

"I don't. I don't ever have to eat when I'm with you, John Savage."

He took her hand, and they walked out of the shadows and headed for the firelight. The sparks were like golden fireflies rising in the smoke and vanishing like tiny suns in the darkness.

"Come on, John," Ben called when Eva

and John walked into the circle of golden light. "Time for our pie social."

"Ben must have talked your ma into something," John said.

"Love is in the air," Eva said, and danced away like a graceful ballerina skipping rope. She got two bowls and stood in line behind Whit, glancing at John, giving him a coy smile.

The wagon with Pepito and Carlos rumbled up, and they parked it alongside the chuck wagon. Emma and Ben headed for a log and sat down together, wooden spoons in hand. The firelight revealed the blush on Emma's face.

Whit sat off by himself and ate his stew. John and Eva sat on the ground with Gasparo, Manolo, Carlos, and Ornery. Pepito and Juanito sat near the chuck wagon, putting their bowls atop their guitar cases. Corny sat down last, next to John, his bowl steaming with savory aromas. He dipped his spoon in the broth and burned his tongue when he put the stew in his mouth.

Everyone laughed.

"You might want to blow on that, Corny," Dobbins said. "I ain't 'sponsible for burnt tongues."

"It's better tastin' than my granny ever made," Corny said.

The laughter and the banter continued until the meal was over. Then Pepito and Juanito tuned up their guitars and started strumming a lively Mexican tune. They moved to the wagon sheets, which were bucked up together in front of the cabin.

"Vamos a bailar," Pepito announced. "Everybody dance."

"Shall we?" Eva said to John as she took his bowl and set it inside hers.

The two musicians were playing a furiously fast tune.

"The only way I could dance to that would be to drop a hot coal down my britches," he said.

"Oh, come on," she said, standing up and pulling on his hand. "I'll teach you."

"Oh, so you're going to be my teacher," he said, and allowed himself to be jerked onto the makeshift dance floor. Eva's feet flew on the wagon sheets and she guided John through intricate steps, hiking her skirts when she whirled away from him, dropping them only when she returned to take his hands.

The guitar players varied their tunes, playing some slow, some fast, some mournful and sad. Dobbins brought out his squeeze box and added to the joyfulness of the occasion.

Carlos and Gasparo danced together. Manolo danced with Emma, and so did Corny. John danced with her, too, while Whit danced with Eva.

"I see you and Eva are getting acquainted," Emma said to John.

"She's a nice young lady."

"See that you keep her that way," she said.

"Whoa, Emma," he said. "I don't see a chaperone's bonnet on your head."

"She's just a young girl, Mr. Savage."

"Why don't you call me John? And I know she's young. And sweet and innocent."

He whirled her in time with the music, his dark eyes locked on hers, his jaw set in a hard line.

"Just be careful, John. I don't want you to break her heart."

"You can break a leg jumping to conclusions," he said, twirling her in a tight turn.

"You dance so harshly," she said. "I'm getting dizzy."

"Harshly?"

"You're an aggressive dancer, John."

"Maybe you want to try a waltz, Emma."

"The music is just fine, I just don't like to be tossed around like a rag doll."

"Maybe I should warn you about Ben," he said.

"What's wrong with Ben?" she asked, her

eyes opening wide.

He leaned close to her and whispered.

"Ben can't dance, either," he teased.

"Oh, you," she said. "Ben is a very good dancer. And a very polite man."

"I taught him manners."

"You're a big tease, aren't you, John?"

"When I'm happy, I can be," he said as the music faded away. He bowed to her and led her back to Ben.

"She's all yours, Ben," he said. "Emma wore me out."

Ben scratched his head as John walked away, back to Eva.

They watched the dancers.

"Your ma has her eye on us," he said.

"John, let's not dance anymore. I'm — I'm tired."

"The night is young," he said.

"I'm going in to bed," she said, and squeezed his hand. "Make sure Whit sleeps with you and Ben tonight."

"Eva, what's the matter?"

"Just do that for me," she said. "I'll tell you later."

Eva ran to the cabin. John looked at Whit, who was watching his sister, a peculiar look on his face.

When Whit turned around, John beckoned to him.

"Yes, John, what is it?"

"Whit, I want you to ride down to the trail that leads to the creek we're panning and spend the night. Take your bedroll with you and a pistol."

"You want me to guard the trail?"

"Yes."

"Where you gonna be?"

"I'll bed down in the trees with Ben and Corny."

"All right."

"Whenever you're ready, Whit."

Whit walked over to Ben and his mother. John saw Ben unstrap his gunbelt and give it to the boy. John knew he had another rig in his saddlebags.

Later that night, when he and Ben were laying out their bedrolls, Ben whispered a question to John.

"How come you sent that kid to guard the trail up here, John?"

"I don't know, Ben. It's something I have to figure out."

"You are just full of mystery, Johnny. Plumb full of pure mystery."

"Go to sleep, Ben."

John lay down and looked up at the stars through the trees. He thought of Eva and what she had said about Whit.

A light had come into his life, and now
somebody had put a shade over it.

23

Thatcher bathed his sore foot in horse liniment, his face greasy with sweat from sitting too close to the fire.

The creek basked in morning mist, all but invisible to the four men who sat around the fire, munching on hardtack and jerky, drinking almost scalding coffee from tin cups. The only sounds were the raucous calls of jays flitting through the aspens and the pines, and the soft whickers of their horses as they grazed, hobbled, in the timber.

"This coffee tastes like it was boiled with your socks, Harry," Krieger said.

"I made it same as usual," Harry said.

"I don't taste no cinnamon in it," Ferguson said. "And it don't taste like Arbuckle's."

"Cinnamon dropped in the pot yesterday," Short said. "You're tastin' the rye whiskey you guzzled last night, Al."

Short blew the steam off the top of his coffee and took a swallow.

"Tastes all right to me."

"It tastes like it's got horseshit in it," Krieger said. But he took another sip and swallowed it. His eyes were red-rimmed and his head throbbed like it had a trip-hammer pounding at his temples.

"More like owl shit," Ferguson said. "And I didn't drink no rye last evenin'."

"You and Old Taylor were good friends last night, Walt," Thatcher said, wincing as he felt his swollen ankle.

"That foot of yours is so red, it could light the whorehouse district in Cherry Creek," Ferguson said. "You might want to wrap it with gauze or cut the damned thing off."

"You a sawbones now, Walt?" Thatcher cracked. "I don't see no shingle hangin' from your tent."

"I hope to hell you did some tall thinkin' last night, Lem," Ferguson said. "None of us can take much more of these dry diggin's."

"Keep your hat on, Walt," Thatcher said. "I did some thinkin', all right, and I'm doin' more of it now."

"Seems to me you kept your cup pretty full of Old Taylor last night yourself, Lem."

Ferguson watched as Short busied himself

laying out a flat piece of board and unpacking the weighing scales. Harry was the only one doing anything useful that morning, with the chill still on the land and the mist so thick, it made a man think of San Francisco and the Embarcadero.

"Harry," Thatcher said, "we got any bandages?"

Short looked up from the scales where he was weighing gold dust. The scales sat on a square board lying flat on the ground.

"Yeah, in the medicine box."

"Bring me a roll, will you?"

"Sure, Boss," Short said, and stood up, careful not to disturb the board and scales.

"Don't nobody touch them scales," he said, as he walked to one of the pup tents. He dropped to his knees and crawled in. He backed out on his hands and knees, pulling a small wooden box. He took it over to Thatcher, who opened it.

He pulled out a roll of bandages still wrapped in butcher paper. He began wrapping his ankle with the gauze. When he had the bandage tight and thick, he used both hands to tear it. Then he split it down the middle, using nearly a foot of the material, wrapped that around the bandage, and tied two strong knots in it. He put the roll back in the box and closed it.

"You can put it back now, Harry," he said.

Harry, who had been looking on, picked up the box and carried it back to the tent. He knelt down and shoved it inside. Then he squatted back down with his scales and poured a pouch of gold dust into one of the copper baskets. He placed a square chunk of lead in the other. The bowl of dust sank and he added another chunk of lead.

"Four ounces," he said. "That's what three of us panned out today."

"And yesterday we got only two ounces," Ferguson said, glaring at Thatcher.

"It adds up," Thatcher said.

"Not fast enough," Krieger said, who was poking the sand with a stick he had whittled from an aspen branch. "And mighty poor pickin's. I've shoveled enough gravel into that sluice box to build my own pyramid and not enough dust to cover the head of a pin."

"My back's so sore from pannin'," Short said, "it feels like I got the rheumatiz. And my legs feel like they been mashed with a pile driver."

"How much panning will you do today, Lem?" Ferguson asked.

"I'm crippled up, Walt. You know that."

"So, you're just goin' to lie around camp while we uns break our backs shovelin' gravel into the sluice box or swirl sand around in a pan."

"I had something else in mind, Walt."

"Let's hear it, Lem."

"See that fog on the creek?"

"Yeah, I see it. You can't miss it. Thick as Grandpa's whiskers."

"It hides the creek, and it can hide us now and again."

Ferguson finished his coffee, threw the grounds out with a whisk of his cup.

"Hide us from what?"

"I got me a plan," Thatcher said. "All of you sit up and listen."

"We're listenin'," Krieger said.

"Yeah," said Short.

Ferguson set his empty cup down and pulled his legs up, set his arms and head on his knees.

"Any of you ever heard of the Swamp Fox?" Thatcher asked.

Krieger and Short shook their heads. Ferguson nodded.

"Civil War general, warn't he?"

"Brigadier general," Thatcher said. "He changed the way soldiers fought in the Revolutionary War. Snuck around, hid out, and picked off British regulars whenever he had the chance."

"What are you getting at, Lem?" Fergu-

230

son said, raising his head and stretching out his legs.

"That fog gave me the idea," Thatcher said. "We can fight this Savage feller and beat him. All we have to do is keep our wits about us. I propose that we break camp and take to the woods. My great-granddaddy fought with Francis Marion, the Swamp Fox, and he told my grandpa and my grandpa told my daddy and he told me how old Marion outfought and outwitted the British. Why, he's still a hero back in Georgetown, South Carolina."

"We ain't but four of us, Lem," Krieger said. He looked at Short. "How many Messicans did you count, Harry?"

"Half a dozen, maybe. They was still drivin' in cattle when I left."

"Numbers don't mean nothin'," Thatcher said. "I say we scout that tabletop. Let's say he has nine or ten Mexicans. Then there's Savage, his partner, Corny, maybe a couple of settlers, and that snot-nosed Blanchett boy. When we know where they live and sleep, we can pick 'em off, one by one."

"And have Savage trackin' us down," Krieger said.

"We use the tricks of the Swamp Fox," Thatcher said. "We cover our tracks. We wipe 'em out. We don't camp in the same place two nights in a row. We shoot, we kill, we hide."

"That might take all summer," Ferguson said.

"Might, but I don't think so. If we can kill Savage, we cut off the head of the snake. Them Mexicans will run like rabbits if Savage goes down. I tell you it can be done. By God, we'll do it. We'll break camp right now and hide in the woods, up next to that flat valley."

"What do we do for food?" Short asked.

"Live off the land, like our grandparents did. There's plenty of game up here. Mule deer, elk, partridges, quail, rabbits."

"You're crazy, Lem," Ferguson said. "Plumb crazy."

"Am I? Or am I just smarter than you, Walt? Who grubstaked you?"

"You had to kill a man to do that, Lem."

"And what's a few more men to get what we want? Savage is getting rich on his claim. We're suckin' hind tit at ours."

"It might be a good idea," Krieger said. "We're all good shots. We can sure whittle down the odds over time, I reckon."

"You're damned right, Al," Thatcher said. "That's the idea. And say we don't get Savage right off. We got dynamite. Comes to that, we can blow him out of his mine, blow him off the bank of this here creek. Him and his partner and that whippersnapper of a kid."

"Let's do it," Krieger said. "I'm tired as hell of sluicin' and pannin' and gettin' nothin' but pennies for my work. I'd like to get our rifles back from Savage and see him shot or blown all to hell."

"I'm game," Short said.

Thatcher looked at Ferguson. Ferguson stood up.

"Count me in," he said.

"Then, let's get to it," Thatcher said. "Harry, go round up the horses and we'll start striking our tents. We can leave most of the tools, the sluice box and such. Travel light."

In an hour, the tents and gear were packed, loaded on panniers, and the four men were mounted on their horses. They traveled north along the creek, and climbed into the thick timber that bordered the tableland where Savage was building his cattle ranch. By nightfall, they had found a camping place next to a rocky outcropping, high up in the timber. They pitched their tents and the next day, they hunted north of their camp.

By noon, they had a mule deer hanging from a pine limb, all dressed out and skinned. They built a fire pit and feasted on venison that second night.

The next morning, they drew blades of grass to see who would be first to scout the grassy plateau. Thatcher selected the stems and held them in his fist.

Krieger drew the shortest blade of grass.

"I want you to count heads, see where Savage is, what the Mexicans are doing, and how many men are carrying arms. Got that, Al? Take a spyglass with you. And don't get caught."

"I'll have to blaze my trail to find my way back here."

"Small blazes," Thatcher said. "High up or low down."

"Low down, I reckon."

"High up is best," Ferguson said. "Men tracking don't look up, they look down."

"You'd make a good guerilla fighter, Walt," Thatcher said.

"I done some trackin' in my time," he said.

Krieger left on foot late that afternoon. He was packing a six-gun, a Henry .44, hardtack, venison, a wooden canteen full of springwater, and a telescopic spyglass.

He walked six miles through the woods, standing on tiptoe to blaze his path. When he saw the valley and the cattle, he searched for a hiding place somewhere along the northern edge of the plateau. He crawled to a thicket of brush and lay flat on his belly. He set a rock in front of him, and rested the spyglass atop it. He began to scan the valley, marveling at the grazing cattle. He heard men chopping down trees, saw others notching logs and setting them up, while another man rode a wide circle around the herd.

He saw two women washing clothes in large tubs outside the cabin, and hanging the clothes on a line to dry. Later, he saw the two tending to their garden, and his stomach churned with hunger.

There was no sign of Savage or his partner, Ben. Nor did he see young Blanchett, but thought he might be in the woods helping to chop down pine trees.

He counted the number of men he saw, scratched parallel and vertical lines in the dirt. One, two, three, four. Horses skidded the logs out of the timber. Four men, two women. Then, a fifth man emerged from the woods. All were Mexicans.

No sign of Corny, either.

Perhaps, he thought, Savage, Corny, that Ben, and the boy were working their claim down on the creek. There was no way to tell, but he added four more lines, for a total of nine. He drew a line through the first four on a slant, which counted for five men. Then he had four standing lines, not counting the two women.

A lot of people to kill, he thought.

And what about the two women? Would Thatcher want to rub them out, too? No need. And through his spyglass he could see that they were both comely women. No, they could be spared for other things. Things a man might want after spending days or weeks in the wilderness.

Krieger had many thoughts as he watched and waited for nightfall.

Perhaps, he thought, Thatcher's idea was sound. It would be easy to pick off the Mexicans. Maybe two or three at a time. That would cut down the odds.

But there was still Savage and his fast draw to consider. At long range, though, a rifle could bring him down. Then there was Thatcher's idea of the dynamite. If they could pull that off, they'd be sitting pretty, right smack on top of a producing gold claim.

Sure, there might be a lot of dead men, Krieger thought.

But dead men told no tales.

It all seemed so easy to him as he lay there in the cool shade, completely invisible to those he watched. Men who would soon be dead.

24

John could make no sense of the dream, although it seemed very real to him.

The dream was filled with metal objects, contraptions that did not work, and there were dark men on horseback crossing a shining stream. A young woman called to him from a high rock on a mountain that appeared to have been plowed to raw dirt. The girl held out her arms to him, and he struggled up one of the furrows with something like a bow and arrow in his hand, but the objects turned into steel braces that would not fit beneath a wagon that suddenly appeared out of nowhere. The shadowy men were riding down the furrows, shooting golden rifles at him, and he could hear the bullets sizzle past him like a flight of angry bees. He picked up a stone that changed into a mangled pistol. The bullets fell out of the cylinder and he kept trying to stuff them back in, when the gun turned into a broken clock, its springs sticking out, its mechanisms twisting into grotesque shapes when he tried to cram them back into the wooden shell.

He heard the woman call his name, but her face turned away from him, and when she turned back it was Ben, or someone resembling Ben, and he slumped over and turned into a wolf, trotting away over the mountain until he was swallowed up by blinding white snow.

A door opened, and John heard someone whisper his name. He saw a shape in the doorway, and it was his sister. His sister was calling to him, "Johnny, Johnny," and he opened his eyes in shock, jerked out of the dream by someone tugging on his hand. He felt the whisper of mist on his ear, the heat from an open mouth, and a pigtail dropped on his chest like a snake.

He sat up and there was Eva, holding a finger to her lips.

Ben was sound asleep, his soft snores sounding like a muffled throng of tree frogs.

She moved away and beckoned to him. He saw her by moonlight, walking between two trees out onto the plain, the grassy plain that glowed a soft pewter under the gauzy light of the moon and the stars. He arose from his bedroll and followed her to a place near the garden. She turned and beckoned to him again. She was wearing worn-out trousers that might have been her brother's and a faded denim shirt that was too large and must have been her father's. Her pigtails fell over both shoulders, so that she looked twelve years old instead of twenty.

"What is it?" he whispered.

She sat down, curling her legs beneath her, and held out a hand.

"I want to talk to you," she said.

He rubbed the grains of sleep from his eyes and sat down. She grabbed his hand, and he saw that hers was shaking.

"What's the matter, Eva? What time is it, anyway?"

"It's after midnight," she said. "I couldn't sleep. I had to talk to you before morning."

"Are you scared? You're shaking like a leaf."

"I've been scared all night, John," she whispered. "I'm glad you sent Whit far away last night."

"Why?"

"What he said and did to me on the dance floor."

"What was that?"

"He warned me to stay away from you. He — said I was his and he would have me. He pinched my bottom and — and he fondled my breast."

"Are you sure?"

"John, he said he was going to do to me what my pa was going to do."

"Your pa? What was he going to do?"

"He was trying to rape me. He snuck into my room the night before he left. And he was naked and he — he pulled the covers off me and I could feel him between my legs."

"Did he . . . ?

"I jumped away. He was drunk. I ran outside and hid in the woods until morning. But Whit knew what had happened. He was watching."

"And your ma?"

"She never mentioned anything, but I think she knew. In her heart of hearts, I think she knew."

"So, like father, like son," John said.

Eva nodded.

"You've got to keep him away from me, John. Take him back to the creek with you. I don't want his filthy hands on me."

"He won't touch you, Eva. I'll see to that."

"You've got to, John. I'm scared to death of Whit."

"I'll keep him busy at the diggings, but I can't watch him all the time."

"I know. But if he gets me alone . . ."

241

"I understand. Don't worry. I won't let that happen to you."

"You're a good friend, John. And kind. I want to save myself for . . ."

She didn't finish, but John's heart pumped fast and he could feel the blood pound at his temples. Eva was a very desirable young woman, and to think that her brother wanted to deflower her was more than he could bear. He had to make sure that Eva was safe, and if he was any judge of character, that would take some doing.

"You go back to bed," he said. "Get some sleep. Don't worry about a thing."

"I-I won't. Not with you watching over me."

She threw her arms around his neck and kissed him. Hard. He felt a tug of desire and then, suddenly, she released him and was gone, dashing to the cabin, her bare feet flashing in the moonlight. He sat there for a long moment and wondered if he was still asleep, still dreaming. He stood up and walked back to his bedroll.

The clouds were low in the sky, and he knew there would be fog on the creek. There was plenty of work for his men, who would be building a bunkhouse and quarters for him and Ben. The chuck wagon was full of stores, and the men could shoot game for the larder. They were good for a month or more, he reasoned, before he'd have to send a wagon into Denver for supplies.

He walked back to his bedroll and sat down, looking at Ben, who was still snoring softly, his mouth partly open, his hat crumpled up beneath his head. John reached under his blanket and pulled out his pistol and holster, strapped it on. He knew he could not go back to sleep, not with all that was on his mind.

He woke Ben an hour later, while it was still dark.

"Huh? Wha . . . ?"

"Time to get cracking, Ben."

"Mmm, what for?"

"Got to make some money. At the creek."

"Aww, John, it ain't even light yet."

"We'll see daybreak from the saddle. Come on."

John furled his bedroll and tied it in back of his saddle. He was mounted on Gent by the time Ben came stumbling up to Rusher. He could hear Ben grumbling under his breath until he pulled himself aboard his horse.

"Ain't we even goin' to say good-bye to the ladies, John?"

John didn't answer. He had already said good-bye to his lady, if he could call her that, and he didn't want to stir the entire encampment. They rode through the filmy shrouds of mist and clouds, past bedded-down cattle. They both waved to one of Carlos's men, who was walking the edge of the plateau. He waved back, his rifle slung over his shoulder.

"We ain't taking Corny with us?" Ben said.

"No, just Whit."

"That ain't a fair exchange."

"I want you to keep your eye on the kid, Ben."

"Hell, I ain't no nursemaid."

"I'm going to be watching him, too. I don't want him sneaking back to his ma's, day or night."

"Sneaking?"

"Well, he snuck away to go down to the camp of those claim jumpers, didn't he? I'd call him a sneak."

"Hell, he ought to be up here helpin' with the work. We don't need him."

"No, we don't. But neither does Eva."

"What's Eva got to do with it?"

John told him.

"Well," Ben said, "he's a growin' boy and I have heard him tuggin' on his tallywhacker at night. Like any young kid, I s'pose."

"What he wants to do with his sister is not normal."

"No, it ain't. I knowed there was some reason I didn't like that kid. Too much like his pappy, maybe."

"Maybe," John said. "Not a word to Whit. Just keep your eye on him."

"There you go again, makin' me into a nursemaid."

"If he touches his sister again, Ben, I'll kill him," John said.

"You keep on, you'll whittle that Blanchett family down to a nub."

"I guess you got a right to know, Ben. I'm sweet on Eva."

"Hell, that's plain to see. And she takes to you like a duck to water."

"I can't see ahead, but I want . . ."

"Want what?"

"Never mind. That's between me and her."

"Fine with me. I don't like to mix in folks' private lives nohow."

Whit was still asleep when Ben and John rode up on him. The sky was broken open and filling with a cream light when Ben hopped down and booted the young man awake. Soft, blue-gray clouds streamed across the eastern horizon as the rent opened wider. The clouds on the plateau drifted upward on the morning breeze, and the mists were spindly tendrils along the creeks. They heard the moan of cattle and the distant croon of an owl.

"Shake a leg, kid," Ben said as Whit sat up, rubbing his eyes.

"Where we goin'?" he said, as he looked around, seemingly unsure of where he was. He reached back and rubbed one of his shoulder blades. "I must've slept on a rock. My back hurts."

"It'll work out once you're in the saddle," Ben said.

In moments, Whit was in the saddle, following Ben and John down the trail to the creek. He was still half asleep, and held on to his saddle horn with one hand to keep from falling. He shrugged and twisted his back to get the shoulder blade back to normal.

John was relieved to see that their camp was untouched. But there were fresh boot tracks in the sand. After they all hobbled their horses across the creek, Ben and John walked to the string of pebble-filled tin cans. John examined the ground beyond the warning barrier.

"Two men were here," he said. "Probably yesterday. One walked to our camp and came back. The tracks lead to their diggings."

"Sure looks like it," Ben said.

"I'm going up there and scout them out."

"By yourself?"

"No use making a parade of it, Ben."

"You could be in trouble. One man against at least four."

"You keep your eye on Whit. Put him to work on that rocker."

"I'll put on my maid's bonnet and get out the feather duster, Master."

"You're funny, Ben. Real funny."

John slung his Winchester over his shoulder and started walking north along the creek. Ben watched him go until he disappeared.

"Man's like an Injun," Ben muttered to himself. "He don't make no more noise than a damned ant."

He returned to camp and put Whit to work on the dry rocker, while he himself set up the sluice box and grabbed a shovel.

Two hours later, John returned. Neither Ben nor Whit heard him walk up, and they both jumped when he spoke.

"Ben, I think something's up with those claim jumpers," John said. "They packed up and left, lock, stock, and barrel."

"What?"

"Their claim is clean as a hen's egg."

"Ha," Ben exclaimed. "Their diggin's petered out and they went back down to Denver or Cherry Creek."

"No. I followed their tracks for a time. They tried to brush them out, but they didn't go back to town."

"Where'd they go?"

Whit had stopped shaking the rocker and was listening to every word.

"Up in the timber, far as I could tell."

Ben scooted his hat off to one side and scratched his head just above his left ear.

"That don't make sense, less'n they aim to be hard-rock miners somewheres."

"Those men aren't miners or prospectors, Ben. They're claim jumpers. And probably killers. Like the ones who killed my family and your brother and all our friends."

"Damn."

"My guess is that they know about our ranch and they want to drive us off, take our claim and everything we have."

"John, that's serious."

"You're damned right it's serious."

"So, what are you going to do, John? What can we do?"

John drew a deep breath and looked at the flowing waters of the creek, the dancing butterflies that skipped through the air like yellow leaves in fall, the sun glancing off the riffles and sprinkling diamonds in the eddies. He had once seen that same creek red with blood, his mother's blood, his father's blood, and his sister's.

He wasn't going to let that happen again.

25

John realized that all his dreams, the serenity and contentment that were part of this place in the Rocky Mountains, were about to go up in smoke, or be drowned in blood. Those feelings had evaporated when he saw the tracks leading into the timber. Now they were being replaced by a fierce animal inside him, something that was growing claws and fangs and razor-sharp teeth.

"Well, John," Ben said while John was gazing at the creek, the sky, the white-barked aspens, the green pines, the spruce and fir trees. "Do you know what you're going to do, what any of us is going to do?"

John's lungs filled with the cool fresh air of morning, and he looked long and hard at Ben.

"I'm going to get Gent and track those bastards, Ben."

"And if you find them, then what?"

"I don't know. I'll make that decision

when the time comes."

"I'll go with you."

"No. You and Whit stay here. Keep your eyes open. If I'm not back by sunup tomorrow, you ride up to the Blanchett place and warn everybody that there might be trouble."

"What about me, Mr. Savage?" Whit said.

"If Ben has to leave, you stay here, if it's safe."

"I don't want to be here by myself," Whit said.

"It's not a good idea, John. Leavin' the kid here alone."

John threw his head back and breathed air through his nostrils.

No, it was not a good idea. The kid probably couldn't defend himself, and if Thatcher and his bunch came back in force, Whit might be killed. John realized that he was in a quandary. He wanted to keep Whit away from Eva, but he couldn't just abandon him to the wolves that might come swooping down on their claim at any time.

"I tell you what, Whit. If Ben leaves, you go with him. But you stay away from Eva. If you so much as lay a hand on her, I'll kill you dead without a second thought."

"I-I — what do you mean, Mr. Savage?" Whit stammered.

"You know damned well what I mean."

Whit hung his head and started shaking with rage.

John turned to Ben.

"If he chases his sister around the bed, Ben, you shoot him. Got that?"

"It would be a pleasure, John. Now you know where you stand, kid."

"I-I-y-you got no right. I ain't done nothin' to Eva."

"What I hate most is a liar," John said. "Eva's scared to death of you. She was scared to death of her father. So don't deny your intentions, boy. Just shut up and keep your nose clean and you won't die young. Got that?"

"Y-Yes, sir," Whit said, his eyes misting with tears.

"You got grub in your saddlebags, John," Ben said. "We ain't et no breakfast."

"I got jerky and hardtack, some dried apricots. I'll get by."

John started across the creek to get his horse. At the water's edge, he turned to Ben.

"Cache all our pans and picks before you leave, Ben. Thatcher and his bunch might just come back here."

"You don't expect to make it back by mornin', do you, John?"

"Just be ready for anything, Ben."

Ben and Whit watched him wade across the creek and disappear into the timber. Moments later, they heard Gent moving through the trees, the horse's hooves cracking dry branches and its body crashing through brush.

Then it was quiet, with only the swish and gurgle of the creek, the rowdy squawk of blue jays, and the hawking calls of crows.

Ben felt something go out of him, something lighter than a breath, a feeling of loss. And something heavy replaced it, a weighted sorrow, coupled with a wisp of longing. He wanted to be with John, not with this masturbating boy with lust for his sister in his young heart. Ben and John had been through much together, had lost much, tracked down worse men than Thatcher and his bunch, together, side by side, night and day, winter and summer. And now John was gone and he might never see him again.

"Get your ass movin', kid," Ben roared. "Make that rocker crackle like thunder, you sonofabitch."

And Ben's day went downhill from there.

Whit stayed on the rocker, not even stopping for lunch, and all the time Ben was glaring at him as if he were something poison, something evil.

For Whit, it was the longest day of his life.

26

John forded the creek a few hundred yards north of what had been Thatcher's camp. That was the place where the claim jump-ers had followed a game trail up into the timber. That was as far as he had tracked them earlier that morning. He gave Gent his head and let him follow the tracks along the narrow trail that traversed the slope at an angle. Soon, the trail twisted off into heavy timber, but the hoofprints angled off at that point.

He found a place where one of the men had cut a spruce branch, and later, he saw where the marks that their horses had made had been brushed away. But he could read that sign, too, and he was not thrown off by the tactic.

The tracks were more than a day old, and most had turned dry. Sometimes, there was only a crushed lump of pine needles to show where the horses had passed. There were no blazes on the trees, so he knew they were not going to return to the creek anytime soon.

He was in unfamiliar country, and after a while, when he had determined the general direction Thatcher was heading, he knew he could no longer follow the tracks so closely. They could be waiting in ambush ahead of him, or they could be camped and he might ride right up on them without knowing it.

He tried to think like Thatcher would think, or any man who wanted to hide in the timber would think. They would find a spot for the night, and they would scout other places to camp. They would not stay long in one spot. Chances were that they were still at their first camp and it would be some distance from John's property on the tabletop. But, sure as he was breathing, they would start scouting out his holdings and try to learn all they could about what he had up on the plateau, how many men there were. In short, they would scout the lay of his land and then make their plans.

Now that John knew the general direction Thatcher was headed, he wondered if Gent might not be a liability from then on. He might smell their horses and whinny or whicker. John couldn't chance his own horse giving his position away.

Besides, he thought, if he was on foot, he would have a better chance of getting close when he found their camp. Perhaps he could get close enough to listen to what Thatcher and his men were saying.

He rode on for another half mile, found a place just below a thin ridge that was clogged with deadfalls and rocks and brush. There was grass and a large hollowed-out boulder filled with water. He stopped there, stripped Gent of saddle and bridle, hobbled him. He took his canteen and filled his pockets with jerky, hardtack, a bag of dried apricots, and a box of .44s for his rifle and a handful of extra .45s for his pistol. His gunbelt was full of six-gun cartridges. His knife was still sharp, still caked with steer's blood.

He patted Gent's neck.

"See you later, boy. You wait for me."

He had hobbled only Gent's front feet. If a wolf came after him, Gent could defend himself with kicks from his hind legs.

John munched on a piece of hardtack and a strip of jerky, washed it down with water from his canteen. He climbed the slope at an angle heading northwest. He didn't expect to find tracks right away, but if he didn't after a time, as he drew closer to his own property, he would know he was too high and could start looking for Thatcher at a lower elevation.

John ranged high and low, taking his time, making little or no noise. He found game trails unmarked by iron hooves, examined disturbed earth and overturned pine needles. He listened. Late that afternoon, he heard a man's voice. It was very distant, and muffled, but unmistakably human. He stopped, turned his head in a half circle. Moved a foot and turned his head another 180 degrees.

Nothing.

Had he imagined it?

A man by himself could hear all sorts of sounds in the silence of a forest, or in the emptiness of a town. John had learned not to trust too much at such times. He waited, turning his head, cupping a hand to his right ear.

There, he thought, there it was again. Two voices this time. The voices seemed to be bouncing off something, a rock or a boulder, a bluff. The trees dampened a lot of sound; the leaves soaked up sound or mangled it as it passed through branches. He moved closer to where he thought the sound was coming from. When he heard a man's voice again, he realized it was coming from somewhere below him.

He breathed a heavy sigh. That was good. He was above them.

Were they moving?

He moved closer, stepping carefully, quietly.

He stopped, listened, and heard a voice say: "Good spot."

John couldn't identify the speaker. But he was almost sure it wasn't Krieger's voice. This one was deeper, gruffer, throatier.

He moved from tree to tree, ever closer, until he could hear two or three men talking in low tones. He knew they were staying in the same spot, so they must have made camp. Or they were just resting. But if they were going to scout his property, they would not want to be much higher. Not yet.

He moved still closer, but knew he was still above Thatcher's camp. Something between him and them distorted their voices and made it difficult for him to hear actual words. He just knew there were three or four men talking. But they weren't discussing anything that he could make out. It sounded more as if they were just engaged in some activity that required them to speak to one another.

He saw a large rock outcropping. The sounds seemed to be coming from the other side. From somewhere below it.

John knew he dared not get too much closer. If Thatcher was camped, his men might be scavenging for squaw wood or deadwood to make a fire for the night.

He descended a few yards until he thought he was parallel to the camp. He could see the top of the large rock, like an elephant's shoulder. He heard noises beneath it. He lay flat on his belly and crawled to some bushes and raised his head.

He saw the men and the horses. Or parts of them: a hat, a shirt, an arm, a leg, a horse's rump, another's head and mane, a saddle.

He listened, his head on the ground.

Still, he could not make out the words, but he heard his name mentioned, and someone said the word "Messicans." He knew they were talking about him, his cattle, and his hands.

"Figure about six miles due south from here," Krieger said, and John almost jumped up. It sounded as if Krieger was looking right at him.

"You take that spyglass with you, Al," another voice said. The deeper, gruffer one.

John held his breath.

He heard the word "blaze" and a few more words.

That was enough, he thought. He wasn't

going to go up against four men with only his pistol. His rifle was still in its boot attached to his saddle.

He crawled away, then got to his feet. He made his way back to where he had left Gent. The sun was setting by the time he slid the saddle back on Gent's back.

It was quiet, and he knew he had a decision to make. He could return to the creek, but that was not where he was needed. If he was only six or seven or eight miles from the tabletop, it was about the same distance to their mine above the creek.

He thought of Eva, and realized how much he missed her.

Ben and Whit would ride to the plateau if he wasn't there by sunup. So, he need not worry about them.

He turned Gent toward the south. By his reckoning, he should come out on the tabletop, well above the bluffs. Dead reckoning would take him where he wanted to go.

The sun fell out of the sky and dropped behind the western mountain spires. The timber filled with shadows, and he heard elk moseying through, on their way to feed and drink. He startled a mule deer, who jumped and ran away, scaring Gent, who sidled away and backed down on his rump until John nudged him in the flanks.

The stars appeared and gave John light. He found the Big Dipper and used it as his guide. The peace of the mountains descended upon him and he felt at home. It was tempting to make camp and just bask in the solitude and the serenity. It had always been that way with him. When he went into the mountains, he never wanted to leave. When he left them, it was like tearing off a part of his heart and leaving it behind forever.

He rode on, over deadfalls and through silent pines, stately spruces, and shadowy firs, knowing he was in another world, a world where men had no dominion. There was only the stars and the shining moon and the everlasting mountains, and each moment seemed both fleeting and an eternity.

He did not think of Thatcher and his bunch. He did not think of the past or the future. He surrendered himself to the mountains and let the night claim him. He knew that he and Gent somehow belonged there, with the deer and the elk, the wolves and the owls. This was their country and this was their proper home.

No matter what happened. This was John's home.

27

The thick musky odor of bear scat filled the air as John rode slowly through the shadow-filled timber. Gent's ears stiffened into cones and twisted in all directions. John guided the horse up a ridge that turned out to be steeper than he had thought. He wanted to get away from the bear scent. Spring, he knew, was when bears were hungry and by now, the sows had cubs and were very hostile and protective.

"Easy, boy, easy," John said to Gent as he felt the horse move like an island beneath him, shifting its weight as if it wanted to run, to turn back and flee the cloying aroma that filled its rubbery nostrils.

The tree-lined ridge was wide and steep, a muscled rib that arose from the land like some ancient artifact, the remains of a giant creature that once stalked the earth. There, on the ridgetop, the darkness was intense, and John rode blind through a corridor of trees, with Gent fighting the bit, the reins taut as barrel straps.

Then, without warning, John heard a pounding of heavy feet off to his left. Gent sidled sideways, the bit in his teeth, his neck arched, ears flattened.

With a mighty growl, a large black bear hurled itself out of the darkness, its arms extended, its claws spread like a fan. John felt the rake of the sharp claws down his left leg. The bear gouged furrows in Gent's flank, and the horse staggered under the weight of the charging animal.

John flew out of the saddle as Gent's terrified whinny rent the night with blood-curdling force, then tumbled over the edge of the ridge as Gent galloped straight ahead, the bear's roar in its ears. John heard the galloping hooves for about two seconds as he tumbled downward, somersaulting over rocks and brush. Then, he hit the bottom of a shallow ravine with a thundering crash, and saw the stars spin in the velvet sky just before everything went black in front of and behind his eyes.

A pair of small cubs emerged from the brush and ran squealing to their mother, two furry balls rolling along at high speed.

The bear stood up and roared once more, the sound of hoofbeats gradually getting softer in the distance. Then she dropped to all fours and embraced her cubs before falling to her side to rest and give them suckle.

Far below, John lay unconscious, a lump swelling on his head and blood streaming through the tear in his trouser leg. An owl hooted from a nearby tree and flapped its wings like a crowing rooster. It swiveled its head in silent survey and waited, listening for any furtive sound in the brush below. Its throat pulsed as the scent of fresh blood wafted upward to its nostrils. The owl flexed its talons and sat on its perch, its feathered body a brown sculpture with huge eyes that blinked and focused on anything that stirred its interest. Anything that moved or breathed.

Anything small enough to kill.

28

Ben awoke before sunup the next morning. The cave was still dark and dank from the night dew, and Whit's bedroll was tousled and empty. Ben searched the cave for him, but of the boy there was no sign. When it grew light, he was already across the creek seeing to the horses. The packhorse they had loaned Whit was gone. Corny had the other one, he knew. There was only Rusher and, although he was hobbled, he was still saddled.

No sign of John Savage.

Ben called Whit's name once as he crossed the creek on Rusher. He ground-tied the horse and cached all their tools with the rifles John had taken from Krieger, Short, and Rosset. He left the tents up and rode toward the trail leading up to the plateau. He saw the tracks of the horse Whit had taken sometime during the night.

"The little bastard," Ben muttered, and

wondered if he should now consider the boy a horse thief. "If so," he said to himself, "it will give me great pleasure to hang the ungrateful sonofabitch."

But as he rode up the trail, his thoughts were not on Whit Blanchett, but on John Savage. What had he found out? Had he run into trouble? Was he alive? Or dead? Ben batted those thoughts, and others, around in his brain until he rode up on the tabletop and saw the grazing cattle, the Mexican herders riding through them and counting head.

The high peaks were shining in the sunlight as they towered majestically over the entire back range. The grasses had given off their dew, but the scent still lingered in the air, mingled with the perfume of wildflowers and the heady aroma of pines and spruce trees.

Off to his left, Ben heard a gabble of voices. Men surrounded something large and dark. The men sounded excited as they jabbered in liquid Spanish. They were either arguing, Ben thought, or they had captured a bull elk. He started riding toward them as the men with the cattle galloped toward the group, calling out to their companions.

As Ben approached on Rusher, he saw Carlos break away from the group and step out to face him. Carlos took off his hat and waved it semaphore fashion.

"Ben, you come quick. Hurry, hurry," Carlos yelled.

Ben put Rusher into a lope, then raked his flanks with his spurs until he was galloping toward the confusing scene.

"What's goin' on, Carlos?"

"Come. You see. It is the horse of John Savage."

Ben felt his heart jump, then plunge down into his gut. A nameless fear clawed at him as he saw Gent standing among the chattering men, the burnished leather of John's saddle gleaming like polished teak in the sun.

Ben hit the ground running, leaving his reins trailing and Rusher slowing to a stop.

"Es su caballo," Pepito said to the others.

Carlos had a sorrowful look on his bronze face. His eyes were narrowed, the skin wrinkled at the edges.

"The horse he walk from the trees. He limps. He is much hurt."

"Where's John?"

"I do not know. Just the horse, Ben. Look."

Ben walked to Gent. Gasparo held the reins, but the others were looking at the horse's rump. When Ben saw the deep wounds, his knees turned to gelatin and he sagged a few inches. There were long claw marks and streaks of dried blood on Gent's flanks. He stood hipshot, favoring his wounded side.

"Lord A-mighty," Ben said. "What in the hell happened to old Gent?"

"I think it was a bear," Carlos said.

Ben heard the word *"oso"* several times and nodded.

"That's what it looks like, all right. A damned bear made them claw marks. Show me where you first saw Gent, Carlos."

"Pepito, he see him first. He come through the trees over there."

Carlos pointed to a spot beyond the creek. Some hundred yards off to the right lay stacks of stripped logs, a house halfway built. Other skinned and stripped logs, some already notched, lay beyond the felled trees that had been skidded in by horses. Two horses in harness stood hipshot next to the log structure. Ben looked in that direction as if expecting to see John walking out of the timber. But there was only emptiness. No sign of John. Nothing. His gut rippled with fear; his brain filled with dread. Deep dread. Dread such as he had never known before this one terrible moment.

"You take Gent up to Ornery, see if he

has some salve or liniment in that chuck wagon. Ask Mrs. Blanchett if she can help doctor John's horse. Get that saddle and bridle off of him and put a halter on, tie him to a tree. Make sure he can bed down."

"I will do this," Carlos said.

Manolo stepped up.

"I will lead the horse. Emma, she has the salve."

"I will go with you," Gasparo said.

"What you do now, Ben?" Carlos asked.

"I'm going to look for John. Can you and Juanito come with me? We might be able to backtrack old Gent and find John."

"We will come," Carlos said.

"Say, did you see that Blanchett kid this mornin'? Any of you?"

"We see him," Carlos said. "He come in the dark and we hear bad words in the log house. Then the boy ride off with food and I think he had a rifle."

"Didn't any of you try to stop him?"

"His mother, she scream and yell at the boy, but he just keep riding away."

"Where did he go?"

Carlos pointed to a place up the creek on the same side of the pasture.

"He rode into the timber?"

Carlos nodded. "Yes. He rode fast and we did not have our horses saddled. He just ride away and we no see him. He had the rifle and his saddlebags. They were full."

"Get your horses, Carlos, and let's look for John. I'll talk to Emma later about what happened with her boy."

"She has much anger."

"What about Eva?"

"We no see the young girl. Just the mother. She cry and she scream, and then she go back inside and we no see them."

"Damn," Ben said.

Gasparo and Manolo walked a limping Gent up toward the cabin. Carlos and Juanito walked to their horses and climbed into their saddles. Pepito and Ben walked to their horses.

"I wonder what in hell got into that wet-nosed kid," Ben said, more to himself than anyone else. "Gettin' his ma all riled up like that and just lightin' a shuck."

"That boy, he got much trouble, I think. Here." Pepito pointed a finger at his own head.

"Yeah, he sure does."

Just before the two reached their horses, there was a rifle shot. It cracked like a bull-whip and Ben heard it echo up through the hills. Pepito staggered to one side, uttering a small muffled cry of pain. Then he toppled over, blood gushing from his side like a crimson fountain.

Ben stood there, paralyzed for a moment.

Carlos yelled something in Spanish and jumped from his saddle. Juanito sat his horse, stunned, unmoving.

Ben felt the mountains closing in on him, smothering him, shutting off his breath. His stomach boiled with acid juices and he felt a sickness rising up into his heart, rising like the bile in his throat.

Pepito's horse looked down at him.

Pepito's left leg was twitching and blood poured from a small black hole in his side. Pieces of white rib bones jutted from the bloody mass and there was a pool of blood staining the grass.

Ben saw that much before he could move, and then Carlos, down on his knees next to the fallen man, blocked his view.

But he heard the Spanish words Carlos breathed, and something iron-fisted squeezed his heart.

"Poor Pepito. He is dead."

Ben's world spun on a careening axis, tilted like a crazed carousel, throwing him into a deep dark pit of despair. And the fear snarled in his ear as he heard Carlos sobbing, holding Pepito, and rocking back and forth as if he held his own dead son.

29

Gasparo saw the muzzle flash out of the corner of his eye. The report sounded a split second later. He thought someone was shooting at him. He ducked and drew his converted Remington .44. Manolo twisted in his saddle and saw Pepito fall.

"Cuidado," Gasparo said to Manolo, and cocked his pistol. He began firing toward the brush where he had seen the orange splash of light, but he knew he was too far away to hit anything. And he did not see anyone. But he cracked off three shots and saw the bushes move.

"I think Pepito was shot," Manolo said.

Gasparo turned in the saddle and saw Carlos racing toward Pepito, followed by Ben.

"Quick, Manolo, to the wagon." Gasparo holstered his still-smoking pistol and the two men led Gent up to the chuck wagon. By then, Ornery was outside the wagon, a towel in his hands. The door of the cabin opened and Emma stood in the door looking out onto the pasture.

"Somebody's shooting," she called out, and Eva pushed her through the door and came out to look.

"What's going on, Ma?"

"I-I don't know. Isn't that John's horse with Manolo?"

"I don't know. Look, there's something going on in the middle of the pasture."

Emma looked in that direction.

"Whit," she breathed. "They've shot Whit."

"Oh, Ma, don't be silly. Why would they shoot Whit?"

"I don't know. It's the first thing that came into my mind."

Eva saw Ornery and started toward him.

"What's the shooting about, Ornery?" she said.

"I dunno. But looks like one of the hands dropped out of the saddle. I don't know what Gasparo was shootin' at."

"Whose horse is that?"

She pointed toward Gent.

"Dunno that neither. But it looks a mite lame."

"Oh, Ornery," she shrieked, "what in heaven's name is going on?"

Then Manolo rode up, leaving Gasparo and Gent behind, and he called out to Emma.

"Emma, bring some of that salve you used on your horse's leg when it got cut."

Emma, confused, stared at Manolo as if he had lost his mind.

As Gasparo and Gent came closer, Eva gasped. "Why, that's John's horse," she said to Dobbins.

"Yep, 'pears so, missy," Ornery said.

"Where's John?" she wailed.

"He did not come," Gasparo said. "Only the horse."

"What happened to it?"

"Bear," Gasparo replied as he halted near Dobbins.

Dobbins walked around the horse, saw the wounds.

"I think I got something in the wagon that will help," he said. "First we'll clean those scratches with alcohol and then rub in some medicinal salve."

Emma heard this exchange and recovered her senses enough to go back inside the cabin. Manolo walked over to comfort Eva and help out Gasparo.

"Do not worry, Eva," Manolo said. "We will find John."

He began loosening the single cinch on

the saddle. Gasparo removed the saddlebags and rummaged through them, looking for a halter. Dobbins reappeared with a bottle of alcohol and a tin of salve.

"Manolo, you and Gasparo hold the horse real steady while I doctor him," Dobbins said.

Ben and Carlos carried the body of Pepito over to the unfinished house and lay him under a spruce tree. He looked, Ben thought, like a bloody rag doll, so small and lifeless, his face turning to brown parchment.

"Did you see where the shot came from, Carlos?" Ben asked.

"I think it sound like it come from up there, other side of the creek."

"Yeah, I think you're right. I got me a big problem right now."

"*Un problema,* yes. I think so."

"Do we look for John or chase after whoever shot Pepito?"

"You ask the serious question. I think the one who shot Pepito has run away. I do not know where John is, but his horse leaves tracks, no?"

"We got claim jumpers out to kill me and John, and maybe one of them shot Pepito. John will know what to do. I say we go look for him, follow Gent's tracks. Maybe those bastards bushwhacked John."

"Maybe. I do not like this, Ben."

"Me, neither." Ben could not look at Pepito again. Carlos took a last look and crossed himself.

"Let's get on our horses and find John," Ben said. "Be ready to shoot if you see any of those claim jumpers."

"Now, they are no longer claim jumpers," Carlos said. "They are assassins."

"You are a very wise man, Carlos," Ben said, and they both walked away from the spruce tree and caught up their horses.

They hardly noticed all the activity up by the cabin as they rode into the timber, following Gent's backtrail, hoping they would find John Savage still alive.

Or, Ben thought, find the men who killed him.

He knew that neither he nor Carlos would show them any mercy.

"You see any of 'em, Carlos," Ben said, "you shoot to kill."

Carlos patted his pistol and tapped the butt of his rifle in its boot.

"I do not ask no questions, Ben. I send them to hell for Pepito if John still lives."

"Pepito would like that, I think."

"I would like that, too," Carlos said.

The two spoke no more as they followed

the meandering track of Gent. Dread cloaked Ben's chest in the thick timber, and fear was in his throat and deep in his belly, like some slavering beast just waiting to devour him. If John was dead, so was a part of Ben. He prayed, in his simple way, that they would find John alive and well.

But he would settle for just finding him alive.

30

Whit lined up the sights on his father's Sharps carbine. There, with that bunch of Mexican *vaqueros,* was the man he hated, Ben Russell. The men were moving around, jabbering to one another. He recognized John's horse, but saw no sign of Savage. He didn't care. Ben had mistreated him, kept calling him "boy" and "kid." Well, he wasn't a kid no more, by God, and he'd show all of them: Manolo, his mother, his sister, John Savage. All of them.

Whit held his breath and squeezed the trigger. He had Ben lined up in his sights. The recoil kicked his shoulder. Orange sparks and white smoke burst from the muzzle and the bullet was on its way. A half second after he fired, he realized he had missed. One of the Mexicans had stepped in front of Ben. Whit's heart caught in his throat. It felt as if it had leaped from his chest. Smoke and burnt powder stung his nostrils. Some of the men were looking straight at him. He crawled out of the brush and ran to the packhorse he had taken from Savage. He climbed into the saddle, sheathed the Sharps in its boot, and rode away as fast as he could, the horse dodging trees and rocks and brush. Whit's heart was pounding. He cursed himself for missing the man he wanted to kill.

He was still cursing when he ran straight into Krieger and Short, who halted his horse and snatched the reins out of Whit's hand.

"Well, well, well," Krieger said, "what do we have here?"

"It's that snot-nosed kid we gave a larruping to, Al."

"I know who the hell it is," Krieger said. To Whit, he said, "Looks like you been doin' my job for me, kid. Nice shot. That your daddy's Sharps you got there?"

"Uh-huh," Whit said, clutching the rifle to his chest.

"Gimme that," Short said, snatching the rifle from Whit's hands. "That's a Big Fifty, kid. Much too big for you to handle."

"Hey, maybe not," Krieger said. "Maybe the kid can help us. Would you like to help us, kid?"

"Y-yeah, sure."

"You killed a Mexican. Can you kill a white man?"

"That's what I was tryin' to do. I aimed to shoot Ben Russell. I missed him."

"Maybe you'll get another chance. You come with us, talk to the boss. If he says okay, you'll get your pap's rifle back."

Whit said nothing. The two men braced him as they rode deeper into the timber. After a short while, they came to a camp nestled among some spruces and junipers that grew in a wide circle. The camp could not be seen from outside the ring of trees.

"I heard a shot," Thatcher said, hobbling up to Krieger's horse. "You draw blood, Al?"

"It was the kid here. Killed a greaser."

"Here's his rifle," Short said, handing it down to Thatcher.

Ferguson and Rosset walked over to Whit, looked up at him.

"You're gettin' pretty big for your britches, ain't you, kid?" Ferguson said.

"No," Whit said.

"He wants to kill that Ben Russell, Lem. Said he just missed him."

"Oh, he does, does he? Well, we could use another gun. You trust him, Walt?"

"We can use him, Al. He tries to double-cross us, one of us'll be at his back. One shot and he'd be out of our hair."

Thatcher grinned.

"How'd it look over there, Harry?" Thatcher said.

"Most of 'em are up at that cabin. Heard a lot of yellin' and women screamin'. I think something's happened to Savage. Didn't see him, but the Mexes was leadin' his lame horse up to the chuck wagon. Be hard to make sense out of what's goin' on, and they're probably all real touchy about now."

"Agreed," Thatcher said.

"One down, at least," Krieger said.

"I want Savage," Thatcher aid. "Maybe he'll show up by morning."

"And then what?" Ferguson said, his tone laced with skepticism.

"Then, all five of us start dropping Mexes and anybody else we see."

"That include the womenfolk?" Short asked.

Ferguson shot a hard glance at Thatcher.

"Anything that moves," Thatcher said. "Savage won't have much fight in him once he starts diggin' graves."

"You seem pretty damned sure of yourself, Al," Ferguson said.

Ferguson tapped the butt of his pistol.

"The six-gun," he said, "is the best tool ever invented. Savage won't expect all of us. I have six bullets in here. Every one of them has got his name on it."

"You gonna kill Savage six times?" Ferguson said, sarcastically.

"If that's what it takes."

"I guess tomorrow will tell the tale," Ferguson said. He turned to Whit. "You'll get your rifle back in the mornin'. I hope you drop Ben Russell with it."

"I hope so, too," Whit said, but he did not sound confident.

He felt as if he was in a dream and that nothing was real. But he could smell the sweat of the men and knew that he was among killers. That gave him a thrill, but it also made him afraid.

Deathly afraid.

31

Ben stared at the ground where the earth told a story of the bear attack, the flight of Gent, and a pair of cubs.

"It happened here," Ben said to Carlos. "The tracks tell me that this is where Gent got clawed by a mama bear."

"Where is John?" Carlos asked, looking all around.

Ben dismounted, handed his reins to Carlos. "Let me see if I can figure this out," he said.

He walked across and around the tracks, reading a tale of surprise and flight, of savagery and fear. At the edge of the drop-off, he looked down, saw broken limbs and skid marks where a body had slid downward.

"Shake out your lariat," Carlos said. "Tie one end around your waist and hold on."

Ben started down the ridge slope, holding on to the rope. Carlos braced himself and held on as Ben lowered himself to the bottom.

John lay unconscious atop a smashed fir tree. His hat was gone, his face gaunt and bloodless. Dried blood caked one side of his head.

Ben's heart quickened when he saw him.

"John, John," he called, as he stepped away from the bank and onto a limb.

John groaned, but his eyes did not open.

Ben leaned over him, then ran his hands over his body. No broken bones.

"Can you hear me, John?"

Savage's eyes opened in silent surprise.

Ben's heart skipped a beat.

"Carlos is with me, John. We'll get you out of here. Don't move."

"It feels like my back is broken," John said.

"It ain't."

Ben yelled up to Carlos.

"Bring the horses down here. John's alive."

Carlos peered over the edge, then along the ridge. He nodded.

It took Carlos a good two hours to make his way down off the ridge to where Ben and John waited. John was sitting up, wincing at the pain in his head.

"First thing John wanted to know was how Gent was doin'," Ben said to Carlos.

"He is more scratched up than you are,

284

John," Carlos said.

John grinned, a sheepish look of relief on his face.

He climbed into Ben's saddle. Ben climbed up behind him.

They reached the grassy tabletop at sunset, three weary men and two tired horses.

Eva rushed out to meet them. Emma stood in the doorway, one hand raised in greeting.

Corny walked away from the chuck wagon, carrying a plate of grub. He grinned at John and sat on a stump, his shirt stained with sweat, face washed clean with spring-water.

"Oh, John," Eva cried, "I'm so glad to see you."

He slid out of the saddle and took her in his arms.

"Am I hurting you?" she said, as she squeezed him tight against her.

"Just enough to make me want you to keep doing it," he said.

They walked to the cabin together. Emma stepped aside to let them in.

"Where are you taking him, Eva?" she asked.

"To my bed," she said.

Emma gasped.

Eva gave her mother a wicked smile, and

her chest swelled with a feeling of deep satisfaction.

The moon rose over a hushed land, a land that had already been bloodied.

Men slept, men stood guard. Men waited for morning.

And, sometime before dawn, before the first horse whickered, it seemed to some that time had stood still.

Juanito smoked a cigarette and thought the night would never end, that morning would never come.

32

Walt Ferguson was beginning to think that
Lem might have more brains than a darn-
ing egg.

"That's not a bad plan, Lem," he said.
"Might work."

"I learned something from being at Get-
tysburg, Walt. A better lay of the land than
we had when the federals held the high
ground."

"There ain't no high ground yonder," Ferguson said. "Well, you seen it."

"Yeah, last night told me all I needed to
know. Savage and his hands will all be up
by that cabin. We'll catch 'em by surprise at
first light."

He looked around at the others, Short,
Rosset, Krieger, and the kid, their faces lit
by the orange glow of a low fire. He held a
sharpened stick in his hand, and there was
a bare patch of ground where he had drawn
up his battle plan.

"Any questions before we ride over there and take up our positions?" Thatcher asked.

Krieger spit tobacco juice a good yard beyond the fire. Short wrinkled his lips around a chaw, but didn't say anything. Rosset shifted his weight and pulled a small stone from under his leg, tossed it into the fire. Sparks fluttered in the chill predawn air like golden dust.

"You make it all look easy, Lem," Rosset said.

"It won't be easy, Pete," Thatcher said. "But we have the advantage. They won't be expectin' us and they're all bunched up in one place. You take the first man you see, down him, and we'll swarm all over them like a cloud of locusts."

"They'll be on foot," Short said. "We'll all be on horseback. That should make a big difference."

"And we all got Henrys, 'ceptin' for the kid," Krieger said.

"I wish you'd all quit callin' me kid. That's why I want to shoot Ben Russell dead."

"You show us somethin' today, kid, and I'll call you Mr. Blanchett," Ferguson said. "And you can call me Walt."

Whit grinned and began to feel better. He was clutching his Sharps as if it were a precious possession given to him by a god.

"Put out the fire, Pete," Thatcher said, "and let's get to it. Slow and quiet. It'll be daybreak right soon."

"I can smell the dawn," Krieger said, rising to his feet, using his Henry like a crutch or a cane.

"And it smells like blood," Short said, his eyes glittering like a serpent going after prey.

In moments, the fire was out and they were all mounted on their horses, slipping through the timber like wraiths, their jaws set, their rifles at the ready, their bellies boiling with butterflies and bumblebees.

The pines sighed in the whispering breeze that wafted down from the snowcaps where the mountains stood like ancient citadels in that deep darkness just before dawn.

33

Something ticked in John's brain. He opened his eyes to darkness and moonlight. For a long moment, he did not know where he was, but seemed caught somewhere between a dreamscape and this small room with a beam of gauzy white light streaming through the window. He heard breathing next to him, and saw the dim outline of a face. The face of Eva, her pigtails let out, her hair a dark fan on the pillow. He slid out of bed, and motes danced in the moonbeam like tiny white insects. He bent over and groped on the floor for his clothing, picked up his rumpled shirt and trousers. He put his shirt on, then lifted a leg and stuck it in his trousers, hopping on one bare foot to a chair. He sat down and slid his other leg into his pants. He found his boots and socks, put those on, and reached under the bed for his pistol and holster. He stood up and strapped on his gunbelt.

"John," she whispered, "where are you going? It's still dark."

"Outside," he said softly. "Go back to sleep."

"Mmmm," she moaned, and he saw her turn over and bury her face in the pillow, her mane of black hair blotting her head until it was invisible in the darkness. He felt his head, found the lump where it had struck a rock. Hatless, he walked through the silent cabin and out the front door.

A few feet away, he saw a man smoking a quirly. He walked over to him, wondering who it was.

"John? You rise early," the man said in Spanish.

"Juanito. You stand guard."

"Yes."

"That cigarette gives you away. It glows like a fat lightning bug."

"It is quiet. The world sleeps."

"Where is Ben sleeping?"

"Under the chuck wagon with Dobbins."

"Go get him. Bring him here."

"You will stand watch?"

"Yes. Go on."

Their whispers died on their lips and it was quiet again. John looked at the eastern horizon, beyond the plateau and the bluffs below, to the far rim of the world. A redness was blazing in the east, spreading like a thin crimson scar across a dull grayness of clouds.

"Red sky at morning," John murmured to himself, the lump on his head throbbing faintly as if the ticking that had awakened him was turning into a slight drumbeat of pain. The sky to the east was turning pale, the paleness washing over the stars until they faded and disappeared from the sky.

Juanito returned with Ben in tow.

"John, you after a worm?" Ben said, still rubbing the sleep out of his eyes.

"Huh?"

"You're a dadgummed early bird."

"How's Gent?" John asked.

"I don't know. Probably a mite better'n you after that knock on the head."

"Where is he? I want to see him."

"We got him down in the new house. How's your head?"

"I'll get some powders from Eva later. It's all right."

"You need a hat, too," Ben said.

"All in due time, Ben. Let's go see Gent. Anybody watchin' him?"

Ben looked up at the paling sky, the vanishing stars.

"Manolo should be with him. Ornery rubbed some kind of liniment on Gent's

292

wounds. Cuts ain't too deep. They should scab over in a few days."

"That bear came out of nowhere," John said as the two men started walking across the plain toward the new log house. Juanito lit another cigarette. John heard the match strike and turned to him.

"Why don't you wear a sign, Juanito?"

"A sign?"

"Yeah. One that says 'Shoot me.' You can see the glow of that quirly for ten miles up here."

"Todo el mundo duermen," Juanito said.

"Yeah, everybody's asleep. Not everybody."

John and Ben reached the unfinished structure. Manolo was just inside, by the open door, a rifle in his hands.

"Manolo," John said. "How's my horse?"

Before the man could answer, John heard Gent snuffle and whicker softly through his nostrils. John stepped inside, into soft moonglow and fading starlight. Gent trotted over to him and whickered again.

"I feed him the oats and the corn," Manolo said. "He eat good. Drink, too."

John rubbed the gelding's neck. Gent bowed it even more and John rubbed his topknot.

"Sorry, boy," he said. "But you outran that bear."

He walked around to look at the clawed rump, and Gent sidled away, swinging his rear.

"I'm just going to look, Gent. I won't touch."

The horse smelled of alcohol, liniment, and salve. The scars were covered over with a creamy substance.

"He ain't limpin' no more, I see," Ben said.

"That's a good sign," John said.

"You can ride him inside of a week, maybe."

"I'll walk until he's well," John said.

He and Ben stepped outside into the dawn.

"You keep an eye on him, Manolo," John said.

John looked up toward Emma's cabin. He saw the orange glow of Juanito's cigarette, no other signs of life. The sky was paling fast and the eastern horizon was a smear of blood-red clouds and the blazing tip of the sun.

Before Manolo could answer, a rifle shot rang out, echoing down the valley and up into the hills.

The glowing cigarette spun out of Juanito's hand and cartwheeled to the ground, striking in a shower of sparks. Juanito toppled over.

John went into a fighting crouch, his survival instinct rising to the surface.

Then he saw shadowy riders appear out of the trees, a line of them, each at least one hundred yards apart. They swung down on the encampment firing their rifles, piercing the gloom with flashes of orange light. Bullets thudded into the chuck wagon and one of the supply wagons. Men, roused from their sleep, stumbled out into the open, swinging rifles, tracking down fast-moving targets on horseback.

"Take cover, Manolo," John shouted, pushing Ben out of the way. He started toward the nearest rider, still in a crouch.

"And shoot to kill," he said, drawing his pistol.

"Hey, wait for me," Ben said, drawing his own weapon.

But John did not wait. He broke into a run, his head throbbing with shoots of pain, rifles cracking like bullwhips, bullets whining in the air like angry hornets.

One of the riders streaked toward him, his horse's tail streaming like a dark battle flag. Men cursed and yelled, and John heard a woman's terrified scream that chilled his blood.

He stopped, hunkered down in a fighting stance, and cocked his pistol, held it steady. He held his breath. When the rider was within twenty feet, the man raised his rifle and aimed it straight at John.

Ben called out a warning.

John led the rider, swinging his pistol from slightly behind the man. As the rider aimed his Henry, John saw him disappear over his sights and squeezed the trigger. White smoke billowed from his pistol in a blinding cloud.

He heard his bullet hit home and when he stepped through the smoke, he saw the rider down, his horse galloping away as if it had been snakebit.

John heard another horse galloping toward him from another direction.

Ben shot the horse out from under the rider. Manolo was firing his rifle from the doorway. Bullets whistled overhead from several directions.

John's head thundered with pain as if a hundred kettle drums sounded in his brain.

The man Ben had unseated was not dead. He stood up, his rifle gone, and drew his pistol, aimed at Ben. Fired.

Ben cried out and went down, blood

spurting from his left calf.

"Hold it right there, Savage," the man said, and John recognized his voice.

It was Krieger, and John heard the sound of the man's pistol as he cocked it.

Time stopped for John in that moment, stopped dead in its tracks, as the rim of the sun crept up above the horizon like the angry eye of a god bent on laying waste to all mankind.

34

John squeezed the trigger before Krieger could fire his pistol.

The bullet caught him just above the belt buckle. He doubled over in pain, tried to lift his pistol to aim at John, but couldn't raise his arm high enough. He dropped to his knees as John stepped up to him.

"You bastard," Krieger snarled, his flat lips baring his teeth.

John looked down at him.

"That bullet was Fate, Krieger. The next one is Destiny."

Krieger dropped his pistol in surrender.

"You — you wouldn't shoot an unarmed man, would you, Savage? And I'm hurt bad."

"The hell I wouldn't," John said as he put the muzzle of his pistol tight against Krieger's forehead and squeezed the trigger.

Krieger dropped like a sash weight, his eyes wide in disbelief, already glazing over with the frost of death.

John wheeled and went to Ben, who was sitting down, holding on to his bloody leg.

"You all right, partner?" John said, kneeling down beside him.

"Yeah. The lead gouged out some meat, but didn't break no bone."

"You sit tight," John said, and stood up, racing toward the cabin.

His men were firing rifles and pistols from beneath wagons. Dobbins had two pistols in his hand.

Men fell from horseback, screamed in pain.

One stood up, drew his pistol, aimed it at John.

"You must be Thatcher," John called out.

"How'd you know?" Thatcher said.

"Because you look like the dumbest bastard in the world right now."

"I'll kill you," Thatcher said, gritting his teeth, his face squinching in rage.

John didn't even aim. He shot from the hip and the bullet ripped out Thatcher's throat. He gurgled on the blood and pitched forward like a drunk, staggered a step or two, and then crashed to the ground.

"By the gods, you got the last 'un," Dobbins hollered, and danced toward John. "I got me one, too, and I think Carlos got another."

John looked around. There were at least two dead horses, and men sprawled on the ground like sleepers reaching for something just beyond their grasps.

There was a commotion in the trees behind the cabin. A horse ran out of the trees.

John recognized it as one of his pack-horses.

"What the hell?" he said as he began reloading his pistol.

"They was another shooter what rode up and rode back there," Dobbins said. "It looked like that Blanchett kid."

Emma, stepping from the cabin, heard his words.

"What did you say, Ornery? You saw my son Whit?"

"Yes'm, it sure looked like your boy."

"It couldn't be," Emma said.

Then Eva appeared behind her mother.

"He took Pa's rifle, Ma," she said. "When he ran off."

"I know that, but Whit's not an outlaw like these awful men."

The sun cleared the horizon and the morning sky was a raging scarlet, its fingers stretching across the plateau, lighting up the cattle and the grasses.

John started walking toward the spot where the horse had galloped out of the timber. Dobbins walked beside him, both pistols dangling from his hands. Emma and Eva traipsed after them, both still in their nightgowns and barefooted, hopping as if they were walking on hot coals.

Whit Blanchett was hanging from a pine limb, his head cocked to one side, his young face turning dark brown, his body a sagging weight slowly swinging in the morning breeze.

Emma screamed and collapsed. Eva caught her, held her up.

"Kid hanged himself," Dobbins muttered to himself. "I wonder why."

John took Emma in his arms, patted the back of her head.

"Why did he kill himself, John?" Eva said, tears eking from her eyes, streaming down her face.

"I reckon that boy just inherited too much from his pa's side of the family," he said.

Emma fainted, and John picked her up in his arms.

"You need some smellin' salts, John?" Dobbins asked. "I got some in the chuck wagon."

"Yeah, Ornery, we might need some. Bring it to the house."

As Dobbins started for the chuck wagon, John reached out with one hand, caught his sleeve.

"Say, Ornery," he said, "what's your real first name? I know it isn't Ornery."

"No, it ain't. I was borned in N'Orleans. Me father was Irish and me mither was French. You can guess the moniker they tacked on to me, can't ye?"

"Honoré?" John said.

"I'll get the smellin' salts," Dobbins said, and galloped off like an oversized leprechaun.

"John," Eva said as they reached the cabin, "is it all over? The killing?"

He stopped just before entering through the doorway and looked down at Eva.

"Is it ever over, Eva? There was no reason for any of this."

"Why, John, why?"

He entered the cabin, carried Emma to her bed. She moaned.

"Are you going to answer my question?" Eva said as she sat beside her mother and caressed her face with one delicate hand.

"Why, Eva? I'd say the reason is pure and simple. Greed. That's behind most of the West's troubles. Maybe the world's. Men want things they don't have and don't deserve. They think they can take it from

302

weaker men. And women."

"It's all so senseless," Eva said.

John didn't answer.

It *was* senseless.

And it was going to rain soon and the grass would grow, the cattle would feed, men would be buried, others would heal and go on living. And the mountains would stay the same, old and wise and bigger than anything man could build or steal. That was the way it would be. The way it would always be.